Total-E-Bound Publi

The Fo
Pε

I
Death

The Beasor Chronicles
Gypsies
Tramps

Home
No Going Home

Out of Light into Darkness
From Slavery to Freedom
The Vanguard
Two for One

Anthologies
Unconventional at Best: Ninja Cupcakes

Home

HOME OF HIS OWN

T.A. CHASE

Home of His Own
ISBN # 978-1-78184-579-0
©Copyright T.A. Chase 2013
Cover Art by Posh Gosh ©Copyright January 2013
Interior text design by Claire Siemaszkiewicz
Total-E-Bound Publishing

Published in 2013 by Total-E-Bound Publishing, Think Tank, Ruston Way, Lincoln, LN6 7FL, United Kingdom.

HOME OF HIS OWN

Dedication

Thank you to everyone who loves my cowboys and still asks me about them every chance they get.

Chapter One

Hardin Ranch, Wyoming

"Tony, dinner's going to be ready in ten minutes."

Randy Hersch's voice echoed down the hallway. Tony Romanos rolled over onto his back to stare up at the ceiling. He'd got in early that morning from Las Vegas where he'd finished fifth at the PBR Finals. Not where he'd wanted to end up, but he'd been hurt heading into the first round, so he wasn't complaining too much.

Pounding sounded on his door. "Tony, you awake?" Randy opened the door before stepping into the room.

"If I wasn't, your polite knock would have shot me out of bed." Tony gave his friend a wink as he climbed out of bed. "Let me grab a quick shower and I'll be out in a few."

"Sure. Hey, a letter came in the mail for you." Randy headed out of the room as he delivered the news.

He frowned. No one wrote him and very few people called him either. "Where's it from?"

"Postmark says Texas. Doesn't your family live down there?" Randy stopped, turned and leaned against the doorframe.

"They live in Austin and wouldn't spit on me if I was on fire in the gutter." Tony grimaced as his shoulder ached. His last bull at the finals had jerked his arm and pulled some muscles. He slowly raised his arm over his head to stretch.

"It's postmarked Austin, Texas. Are you sure someone from your family wouldn't write you?" Randy was puzzled.

Tony didn't feel like explaining his family situation to Randy—even though he knew his friend would understand—given what a bastard Randy's father was. "Doubt it."

"Are you done bothering him, love?" Les Hardin, Randy's partner, appeared in the doorway, slipping his arm around Randy's waist.

"I wasn't annoying him. Just chatting." Randy nuzzled Les' cheek.

"I was teasing. Come on, let him get his shower. Margie doesn't like serving cold food." Les threw a grin over his shoulder at Tony as the older man led Randy away.

"Thank you," he mouthed.

Les nodded.

He headed into the bathroom. A hot shower and some good food—that would revive him.

Ten minutes later, Tony joined Les and Randy at the dining room table. He knew they were both curious about the letter he'd received, but he wasn't ready to talk about it. He'd noticed it on the hallway table, but hadn't glanced at it since. If it was from one of his family members, it wouldn't be good news.

"Will you be here for Thanksgiving?" Les spoke up as they began to eat.

He thought about it. Before he had met these two, he'd have found a ranch to work at until the circuit had started up again. Now he knew he was welcome to come and stay for as long as he wanted. Hell, he even had his own room. With the PBR season over, he didn't have to be anywhere.

"I'm heading over to Hawaii for the new all-star event they've started. It'll be done the weekend before Thanksgiving. Think you guys can stand me for the winter?" He took a drink of his beer.

Worry surfaced in Randy's eyes. "We'd never get tired of you. Hell, this is your home now, Tony. We'd never turn you away."

Les grasped his lover's hand. "He knows that. He was teasing." Les' dark gaze studied Tony. "I have a new client coming in this week. She'll be staying for a week or longer. Depending on how well her horse responds."

Grateful for the change in subject, Tony handed Randy the bowl of mashed potatoes. "Does her horse have major problems?"

Les usually worked with a client for a week. That short time was enough to give the rider and horse a foundation to improve upon.

"I think the horse's problem is his rider. She's one of those types who think they know more than anyone else in the world. It's hard on the horse because he's a veteran campaigner." Les shrugged.

"Les and I are moving Lindsay out to San Diego after Christmas. You're welcome to come with us," Randy told him.

Apparently it was Randy's turn to switch topics. Of course, Tony understood why, since Les could spend the rest of the dinner explaining all the things the lady was doing wrong, and Tony had never got the whole English riding rules straight in his head.

"San Diego, huh? Going to get a chance to see Rich while you're out there? How's he doing?" Tony took a bite of his steak while glancing at Randy.

"Good. He'll be here for Thanksgiving." Randy chuckled.

The conversation drifted to general topics and Tony managed to relax, forgetting about the letter for a while.

After dinner, he reluctantly picked the letter up from the table. Randy was right. The postmark was Austin, Texas. He gritted his teeth and looked at the handwriting on the envelope. It wasn't *Tía* Elena's, but it was a feminine penmanship. Elena was the only member of his immediate family who wrote to him, though she was his aunt by marriage. He crumpled the paper in his hand and went through the kitchen.

"I'm going out to the barn."

Les and Randy were washing the dishes. There seemed to be more water soaking their shirts than in the sink. Randy waved to him before leaning in to kiss Les.

"Margie is going to be pissed when she sees the mess you've made of her clean floor." Tony pointed to the puddle on the tile under their feet.

"We'll clean it up later." Les snatched Randy by the waistband of his jeans and jerked their bodies together.

Tony stepped outside, pulling his jacket on. Snow hadn't fallen yet, but Wyoming had been hit with a cold spell. He tugged his hat down tighter and made his way down the brick path towards the small barn where Whiskey Sam, Les' retired show jumper, was stabled. Sam and Sally Jane, the other horses stabled there, looked over their stall doors. He patted them on their soft noses then went on to check the blind colt.

A plaque hung on the colt's door, matching the others in all the barns. 'Blindman's Bluff' was etched on the brass. The black colt eased up to the door, his hot breath bathing Tony's cheek. Those milk-white eyes stared out into the aisle. Tony fed Bluff a piece of carrot he'd grabbed from the kitchen. After eating the treat, the colt moved off out of the stall into his paddock. Bluff would never be a saddle horse because of his blindness, but with his conformation, he might make a good stud. Tony smiled. Les was a good horseman and knew that a handicap didn't mean the colt was useless. There would always be things Bluff could do.

Tony went to the small tack room. After turning the light on, he sat down on one of the trunks that held Les' extra tack. The letter crunched in his pocket. He tugged it out and stared down at it. With a sense of foreboding, he tore open the envelope.

He pulled out a piece of paper. Unfolding it, he scanned down to the signature. Maria. Why the hell was his oldest sister writing him? His hand dropped, hanging between his knees.

He hadn't heard from any of his sisters since he'd run away. He'd never even returned for his other sister's wedding. Of course, Angelina had married the one man Tony never wanted to see again.

He held the letter up to the light and read.

'Dear Antonio,

I would like you to come to Austin and talk to my oldest son, Juan. He is about to make the worst mistake of his life. You are the only one who can stop him.

Your sister,
Maria'

Tony crushed the paper in his hand. He could only imagine what kind of mistake Juan was about to make and he wasn't inclined to go just to be an example of what evil could befall young men. He should have known she had a selfish reason to want to see him. He tossed the letter in a trashcan and stood.

He left the barn, but didn't go inside the house. His friends were silhouetted in the kitchen window, kissing. He didn't want to interrupt them. A neigh came from the training barn. After strolling over to it, he went inside and decided to go for a ride. Maybe it would help clear his head.

He led a sturdy gelding from its stall to saddle him before moving the horse out into the sunlight. He mounted then headed off to ride along the fence.

* * * *

Later that night, Tony sat on the porch, staring out at the shadows of the Rockies. He took a drag on his cigarette. It still amazed him how much Les' ranch felt like home to him.

The sound of the front door shutting made him look over his shoulder.

Les stood, doing a visual check of the paddocks and yard. When Les seemed satisfied everything was right in his world, he turned to pin Tony with a speculative stare.

"I brought you a beer." Les handed him the bottle before settling in the chair beside him.

After twisting the cap off, he took a swig. "Thanks. Where's Randy?"

"In bed. He's taking off in the morning with Jackson for a show in Nevada." Les rested his head on the back of the chair.

"Head hurt?" Tony knew Les' injury seven years ago made the older man susceptible to headaches.

"No. Just tired. All the last-minute stuff for the show, and Randy's dad has been causing problems again." Les grimaced.

"In a fair world, that asshole would be run over by a semi and put out of our misery." Tony shook his head.

"Thank God life isn't fair. I'd have never met Randy if his father hadn't been a complete bastard."

"I guess there's an upside to everything."

They laughed. When a silence fell between them Tony was comfortable with it. He'd never really felt that level of security before.

"So, get good news in the letter?" Les' question was deceptively casual.

Tony chuckled. "I should have known you'd get around to asking."

"Be happy I waited until Randy went to bed. He'd badger you until you told us. I have more patience." Les tilted his head and winked at him.

Tony stood, before wandering over to lean on the porch railing. He pushed his hat back on his head and stared up at the night sky. "It's not that I don't want to tell you guys, but I needed time to work my mind around it."

Les stayed quiet, yet his presence gave Tony the courage to continue.

"I ran away from home when I was fifteen."

"So young," Les murmured.

"Maybe, but I didn't feel like it. My parents gave all their attention to my sisters. They were the golden children." For the most part, he'd got over the jealousy and anger. "I spent a lot of time on my own. Then I figured out I liked boys and I no longer existed in their eyes. They acted as if I'd seduce all the boys in the town."

"Did you?" Laughter rang in Les' voice.

Tony shot him a smug grin. "I'd have tried, but in the end it wasn't worth trying to convince them being gay wasn't an illness."

"Don't blame them. It's hard to be different when there's no one to support you." Les shifted in his chair.

Tony put out his cigarette in the ashtray Margie, Les' housekeeper, kept out for him. He took another drink. Did he blame those boys for doing what society said was right? Not anymore. The only one he remembered was Luis, his first boyfriend, and the scars from that relationship hadn't faded.

"I don't blame them. It was hard, especially in my neighbourhood where everyone knew each other and being different was considered a sin." He heard the bitterness in his words. "I couldn't take it anymore. So at the end of the summer when I was fifteen, I left my parents a note and took off. Got odd jobs where no one asked my age. Survived until I hit eighteen and then joined the rodeo."

Les gripped his shoulder and Tony let himself wish a little. Wish he'd met Les before Randy had. Wish he was a little less loyal and Les was a little less faithful. A hard squeeze and he accepted that fate knew what it was doing when it allowed Les and Randy to meet. Les had the easy-going nature to keep Randy's temper from flying off the handle.

"Have you ever gone back?" Les' honeyed drawl broke into Tony's thoughts.

"No, not even when my youngest sister got married. Figured it wasn't worth the drama. I keep in touch with my uncle's wife. Just enough so she knows how to find me. I sent her your address, since you know my schedule and everything."

"We won't let you run off from here. Randy and I consider this your home."

Les' words touched Tony's heart, but a small part of him knew he wouldn't be happy until he found a love like his friends had.

"The letter's from my sister, Maria. She wants me to come for a visit." Tony tightened his grip around the beer bottle.

"After all this time?" Les frowned. "That doesn't make sense. Did she say why?"

"Yeah. She's worried her son, Juan, is gay and I guess she wants me to talk him out of it, from what I'm reading into the letter."

"Do you think there's something wrong with your parents? Maybe there's another reason why she would ask you to do this," Les wondered.

He shook his head. "*Tía* Elena would let me know if that was the problem."

"Have you decided what you're going to do?"

"Not yet. I've still got that event in Hawaii. I won't go before that, if I go at all. If it's something serious, Maria obviously knows where to find me." He drained his beer. He craved another cigarette, but had made a vow to cut his smoking down. He'd had his last one for the day.

Les hugged him. "Get through the next couple of weeks and come home for Thanksgiving. You can decide then what you're going to do."

Blinking back tears, he said, "I will." He savoured Les' closeness for a minute then stepped back. "Go on inside. You should be with Randy tonight, since I'm sure he'll be gone for a week or so at the show."

"You'll be okay?" Les studied him sympathetically.

"I'll be fine." He would be, eventually.

Les brushed a kiss over his lips. "Goodnight."

"'Night." Another thought of 'what might have been' drifted across his mind as he watched Les walk away from him.

He stuffed the feeling away. No point in wishing on something that couldn't be changed. Randy and Les were perfect for each other. There wasn't anyone else he could see with the young cowboy.

Tony stared into the Wyoming sky filled with bright stars. He'd think about contacting his sister, but for now he'd worry about riding and enjoying his vacation in Hawaii.

Chapter Two

Two weeks later

"Harder."

Staring down into the bright blue eyes of the man he was fucking, Tony grinned. He could do harder. He wrapped his hands around the blond's shoulders and started pounding into him. Mick? Mac? Fuck, Tony couldn't remember his own name at that moment.

The man's lean, tanned body arched under Tony's as his lover placed his hands against the headboard and started to push back. He saw passion glaze those amazing eyes as he nailed Mac's gland.

"Right there. Again." Straight white teeth bit a plump bottom lip as Mac begged Tony to fuck him.

Tony was happy to oblige. One particularly deep thrust and Mac grunted, his ass clamping down on Tony's cock as warm semen spilled between them. He kept rocking, letting Mac's climax milk his own from him. He jerked his hips a few times then froze, filling the condom.

"Fuck," he groaned, locking his elbows so he didn't collapse on the man under him.

Mac's hand shook slightly as he ran his fingers through Tony's hair. "Wow." A satisfied smile lifted his kiss-swollen lips.

"Yeah."

Stunning conversation was beyond him at the moment. His mind had just started to function enough for him to move away and climb off the bed. He took care of the condom then grabbed a washcloth for Mac. After cleaning them both up, he joined Mac in bed. The warm night air danced over his cooling skin. Leaning on his elbow, he looked down at Mac.

"And to think I didn't want to come to Hawaii." Mac laughed.

"It's November in Wyoming. Snow and cold. Hell, I couldn't get here fast enough." Tony chuckled. "Usually, I'm looking forward to the time off, but not the weather." He thought about his nephew, and his sister's request.

"The weather can't be that bad." Mac reached up, smoothing the frown off Tony's forehead.

"Not really. I'm used to it now. I was thinking about old issues rearing their head." He didn't want to talk about his family. "So what are you doing in Hawaii?"

"I was working until today. I'm partners with two others in a personal security service company." Mac trailed his hand down over Tony's chest, teasing his nipples, and smiled at him. "We hire out bodyguards for anyone who needs one."

"If you're one of the owners, why are you here instead of some other muscle?" He played with Mac's blond curls. "Not that I'm complaining or anything."

"Hell, it's Hawaii. Also, I've done some work for the client before and he asked for me again." Mac yawned.

Tony spooned behind Mac, wrapping his arm around Mac's waist. He brushed a kiss over the man's nape. "How about we grab some dinner after a nap?"

"Sounds good."

* * * *

Tony moaned. His dreams had never seemed so real. A warm mouth surrounded his cock, swallowing it down until the head hit the back of his lover's throat. When a set of rough fingers fondled his balls then slipped down to tease over his hole, his eyes shot open. He pushed up on his elbows and looked down the bed.

"Fuck, Mac," he groaned.

His lover glanced up at him, throwing a wink in his direction without taking his mouth off Tony's cock. His hips arched off the mattress when Mac pressed his tongue into his slit. Mac played with his balls and he shivered as Mac eased one slick finger past the muscles at his opening. He bore down, taking the finger deeper. Soon he was fucking Mac's mouth while impaling himself on the fingers inside him.

"God, that feels good," he mumbled.

Mac hummed, the vibration sending pleasure shooting to his balls. They drew tight to his body and he trembled on the edge of his climax. Mac buried three fingers in his ass, hitting his gland in the process.

"Ah," he grunted, coming hard.

His spunk flooded Mac's mouth. The blond drank it down like it was a cold beer after a hot day. Mac kept licking and sucking until Tony's cock softened in his mouth. Tony ran his fingers through the curls resting against his leg.

"You wanting, baby?" He slid his hand down over Mac's shoulder.

"Hmm…a little." Mac nibbled along the line of Tony's thigh, sucking a little bit of skin in.

Tony stretched, and shifted. Mac grunted in surprise when he landed on his back with Tony straddling his thighs. Leaning down, he gave Mac a hard, quick kiss while he reached for the condoms and lube that were close at hand. He smiled as Mac chased after him when he rocked back, foil package and tube gripped tight.

Their moans filled the room, mingling with the crash of waves against the beach outside Tony's condo window. He tore open the foil before rolling the rubber down over Mac's shaft then slicked the man up. He braced a hand on the broad chest beneath him and positioned the flared head against his hole. Mac dug his heels into the mattress and pushed his hips up as Tony lowered himself onto Mac's cock.

"Fuck." The word burst from Tony.

There was a moment of stillness while he adjusted to how full his ass felt. Mac gripped his hips tight, but didn't try to make him move until he undulated his body to encourage a fast, strong rhythm. He slammed down as Mac drove into him. Riding bulls for a living gave Tony a good sense of balance, so he wasn't worried about anything except taking Mac as deep as possible.

Mac wrapped a hand around Tony's leaking cock, stroking him with a rough palm and steady pace. His head dropped forward and their pace sped up, bodies snapping together. Skin slapping skin was one of

Tony's favourite sounds. He tightened his inner passage and milked Mac's cock with every slide out.

"So fucking tight," Mac groaned.

His cock jerked at those words and Tony could feel his climax rocket through him. "Shit." Thick, ropey strings of cum shot from him, covering Mac's hand, stomach and chest.

"Fucking amazing, cowboy." Mac's eyes closed and the most exquisite grimace of pleasure formed on his face.

A few minutes later, he moved to lie next to Mac on the bed. His lover stood and held out a hand to him.

"Let's take a quick shower, clean up and then think about getting food." Mac leered at him. "I don't feel like leaving the condo. Little hard to fuck you out in public, unless you're in to exhibitionism."

Tony laughed and shook his head. "Never wanted anyone to watch me fuck. We don't have to worry about going out though. The friend I borrowed the condo from made sure it was stocked with food. There should be sandwich fixings in the refrigerator."

He leaned over to turn the water on for the shower and Mac squeezed his ass. Straightening, Tony turned and wrapped his arms around Mac's neck, bringing their mouths together. Not many men he'd had sex with liked to kiss. They considered it too girly or too intimate, but Tony loved kissing. He loved the feel of soft skin sliding over soft skin, the heat and wetness of tongues teasing.

Mac nibbled along Tony's bottom lip and he was glad to find out Mac seemed to like kissing as much as fucking.

They stepped under the pounding hot water and cleaned up. After drying off, they tugged on some sweats then headed for the kitchen. Tony made the sandwiches while Mac got the beer. The silence was comfortable. They went out on one of the condo's balconies and sat down at the small table.

Tony opened his beer and took a swig. "Why a bodyguard?"

Mac grinned. "I was in a lot of trouble a couple of years ago. Drugs, gangs and stuff like that. I took off from home, as fast and as far as possible. Ended up living in Los Angeles and managed to straighten myself out. I got a job as a bouncer at a nightclub. I met two guys out there who became my partners in our personal security business."

Tony leered, eyeing the well-muscled body in front of him. "I'd love to have you guarding my body, though I might get distracted by yours."

Mac laughed. "I've had a few of my clients hit on me, but to be honest, the worst ones are the women. I had one who just wouldn't take no for an answer. Kept trying to convince me that one night with her would turn me straight. I finally mentioned the words 'sexual harassment' to her manager. Funny, but we've never gotten work from her again."

"Rough."

"Not really. She was a lot of work." Mac shook his head and stared out over the moonlit ocean. "Some clients are wild. They have money and think that being rich means they can do whatever they want. Others are wild merely because they're strung too tight. They all have secrets and I get a chance to learn them. It's hard knowing and liking them without being able to stop them from self-destructing."

Tony nodded. He'd had a few friends on the rodeo circuit whom he had tried to help, but they had ended up destroying themselves with alcohol, sex and drugs. "It happens to the best of us, I guess."

"What about you? Why ride bulls?" Mac took a swig from his own bottle.

"We have a little more in common than just liking cock." He winked at Mac. "I left home at fifteen, worked at any job I could until I was eighteen. Mostly ranches. When I had the money, I'd go to the rodeo. I loved watching all of the events, but the bull riding was excitement and danger all rolled together. I knew it was what I wanted to try. Turned eighteen and hit the circuit."

"Must have been hard."

He shrugged. "Everyone has times in their lives when things don't go well. I'm not any different than the others. I joined the PBR last year after my travelling partner retired. I crash at his ranch when I need a place to stay. His life partner is a pretty cool guy. He's the one who loaned me the condo." Tony waved a hand behind him at the condo.

"What about your family? Don't you talk to them? I'm heading back home as soon as this job's over to see if I can mend some bridges I burned."

"Hell no. They're the reason I left in the first place." Tony shook his head. "I've got a different family, made up of friends."

He finished his beer before carrying his plate into the kitchen. Mac followed him. They rinsed the dishes and put them in the dishwasher. After grabbing the blond's hand, he led Mac back towards the bedroom.

"There are better things we can be doing than talking."

"I like the way you think."

He buried his hands in Mac's hair, tugging the man's lips to his, thanking God he'd gone to the bar Les had recommended after the final round had finished. He licked along the seam of Mac's mouth and wished he didn't have to go home the next day.

* * * *

Tony groaned as he dropped his bag on a well-used bank of chairs in the Honolulu International Airport and sat down beside it. He glanced at his watch. Shit, he was an hour early. Seven forty-five was way too fucking early for a flight after the night he'd had. The past two weeks had been fun. It was a great way to unwind from the stress of competing. His ass was sore and he smiled, remembering Mac sprawled out on the condo bed. The man's golden skin bore bruises from their night together. Tony shifted on the chair. He wondered if Mac's ass would hurt as much as his did when the man woke up.

He'd done his best not to think about his sister's letter much while he had been there, but he knew he'd have to deal with it soon. He wasn't looking forward to even talking to a member of his family. *Tía* Elena was the only one he liked.

Leaning back, he rested his head on the seat. He was eager to get back to the ranch. His phone rang and when he checked the number, he saw it was Randy calling.

"Hey, cowboy. Tired of that old man yet?"

Randy's laughter filled his ears. "Would you be?"

"No. Les keeps getting better with age. He's going to be sexy as hell when he's eighty." He stood and grabbed his bag. He had enough time before his flight to have some breakfast.

"And for that, I'll be eternally grateful."

Tony chuckled. "So why'd you call me? We talked earlier this morning. Did you miss me? Or are you trying to get details about my hot night of sex?"

"Always. Next to Les, you're my favourite person. You know I'm all ears about your nights." Randy's tone changed. "There's someone at the ranch waiting for you. Les wanted me to warn you."

"Waiting for me?" He was surprised. Anyone who might want to talk to him either had his cell number or knew he was due at the ranch tomorrow.

"Yeah. I just got off the phone with Les. He said your brother-in-law's there."

Tony stopped in his tracks and almost dropped his phone. "Luis is there?"

"He showed up about ten minutes ago. I'm on my way back from town." Randy sounded worried.

"Shit. Did he say anything to Les about why he was there?" Tony glanced around, looking for a spot to collapse.

"No. Just that he was looking for you. Tony, babe, are you okay?" Randy's question was gentle.

"I'm fine. I guess I'm shocked they'd come looking for me." He'd never expected to see Luis again. "Thanks for letting me know. I'll be able to deal with it better."

"Les is going to have him spend the night."

"Don't let him use my room," he blurted out. He didn't want Luis' scent on his pillows or sheets.

"We wouldn't. He can use one of the guest rooms. Will you be all right driving home? Do you want Les or me to come pick you up?"

Tony took a deep breath. *Fuck.* He had to get hold of himself. He couldn't let Randy figure out there might be more history between Luis and him than just being brothers-in-law.

"No. I'll be fine. It's been a tiring trip. I was up most of the night and not thinking clearly. I haven't seen Luis, or any of my family, in over nine years. It's a surprise to have one of them show up on your doorstep."

He made his way to a bar, gesturing for the bartender to give him a beer.

"Okay. I'm home, so I have to hang up. If I learn anything, I'll call you. Let us know when you land in Cheyenne."

"Will do. Thanks, Randy, for everything." He hung up and threw his phone on the bar.

Shit, he was fucking screwed. Why did it have to be Luis who had come to talk to him?

Luis had been the first person Tony had kissed and in his youthful innocence, Tony had thought they'd be in love forever. He'd learnt how to give great blow jobs because of Luis. He still remembered the day he'd suffered his first heartbreak.

* * * *

"Luis! Luis! I did it." Tony burst through the Martinez back door. He knew Luis' parents were gone, so they had the house to themselves.

"Did what?" Luis' bright brown eyes twinkled at him.

He swore he'd never seen anyone more gorgeous than Luis Martinez. This hot guy was his boyfriend, and he had taken the first steps to be able to shout it to the world.

"I told my parents I'm gay. Now we really can be boyfriends."

The look of horror spreading across Luis' face shot ice through Tony's body.

"You didn't tell them I was a fag, did you? You didn't mention my name." Luis grabbed his shirt and shook him.

"No." He could feel tears welling in his eyes. "Aren't you happy? We don't have to hide anymore."

"I'm not a fag, you idiot. You're a nice diversion while my girlfriend's gone for the summer." Luis let go of him and stalked away.

"But you said you loved me. You told me you wished you could tell the world about us." Tony reached for the kitchen counter. Shock and hurt warred in his heart.

"You're as easy as a girl, believing all that shit." Luis laughed. "You give great head, Romanos, but I'm not a fag. Don't expect me to start wearing rainbows and going to parades with you."

* * * *

Tony's heart had shattered that day, but he'd held strong through the gossip and slurs. He'd dealt with his parents ignoring him. For a month, he'd tried to tell himself that Luis would change his mind, that the boy he loved wouldn't throw him away.

He'd been wrong. At an end-of-the-summer party, he'd seen Luis kissing his girlfriend and Tony had realised that even if Luis had lied about not being gay, the boy would never have the courage to admit it.

Tony heard his flight number called and grabbed his stuff. He boarded and put his bag away before sitting. Shutting his eyes, he sighed. Maybe he and Mac should have done a little more sleeping and a little less fucking last night. He was glad he'd upgraded to first class — more room and free drinks.

A nap would help settle his nerves. The memories only served to remind him anyone could hurt him, even those who should have loved him. Someone bumped his arm. Opening his eyes, he saw a tall, lean man sitting next to him.

"Sorry about that. Jackass was in a hurry to get to his coach seat, I guess."

The smooth southern drawl stirred something in Tony's mind. He studied the guy. A blue baseball cap and sunglasses hid his eyes. Tony's instinct told him he knew the stranger.

"Honey, when you get a chance, can you bring me a whisky on the rocks and a beer for my friend here?" The man flagged down a flight attendant.

"Shit. You're…"

"Yeah. Don't say anything. I just want to survive this flight without someone asking for my autograph or a picture." That famous smile flashed at him. "Though I wouldn't mind if you wanted to take one. It's not often such a handsome man recognises me."

Tony's mouth dropped open. There was no way Derek St Martin, country music superstar, was flirting with him.

"If I ask for a picture, wouldn't it blow your cover?" he managed to say.

Derek thought for a moment, his thin lips pursed, then he nodded. "Fuck. Should have known something would spoil it."

"Here you are, sir." The flight attendant handed Derek two glasses. "Is there anything else I can get you?"

"No, sugar. This is just fine." Derek waved her away with a casual gesture.

"Don't you have your own jet?" Tony kept his voice low. He could respect the man's wish for privacy.

"Sure I do, but sometimes I just want to get away from all that bullshit. The entourage, my agent. It all gives me a headache. On good days, I pop a couple of pills and let them take me away. Yet there are times when it all builds up and there's nothing I can do but run." Derek leaned in close to Tony, so close Tony could see the singer's electric blue eyes peering over the top of the sunglasses. "What do you do for a living? You look like a cowboy."

"I ride bulls."

"Mmm…if only that were true, it'd prove there is a benevolent God and he loves country singers."

Tony looked around. None of the passengers seemed to be paying attention to them. He moved closer to Derek. "I like bulls better than cows, but since I've never heard even a whisper about you, you might want to be careful what you say in public."

A look passed over Derek's face and Tony wondered if the singer hated hiding who he was because of his fans. "I know. I've been yelled at by everyone around me. If I promise not to out myself to anyone else, will you talk to me about what you do? Treat me like a real person? Not the stud you see dancing on stage in tight jeans and a T-shirt."

Tony touched Derek's hand where he held on to the armrest between them. "I'd talk to you all day." He pressed his lips to the man's ear. "I've had a hard-on since I first heard you talk."

Derek's eyes widened and he shot a look at Tony's crotch. "Man, what I wouldn't do to have a private plane right about now."

Tony winked, settling back in his seat. "I do ride bulls. I was in Honolulu for the special all-star event."

"Wow. A gay cowboy? So those stereotypes really do exist." Derek laughed. "Are you any good?"

"I finished fifth at the Finals this year." Tony sipped his beer. "Where are you headed?"

"Got a fucking concert in Dallas." Derek drained his drink and waved for the attendant to get him another one. "I got a two-week vacation and then it's back to work. Not even time off for Thanksgiving. It sucks. I planned on going to my brother's house for the holiday, but nope. Have to go entertain the masses."

"Man, if you don't like what you're doing, why are you doing it?" Tony loved riding bulls. He'd already made up his mind that the day he didn't enjoy it, he'd retire.

"I love to sing. Performing is an unhappy side effect of singing. To be honest, I wouldn't be so tired of performing if I didn't have to deal with all the other bullshit." Derek shrugged as he shifted and faced him. "So where are you from? It sounds like Texas to me."

"I'm originally from Texas. I live in Wyoming now." He realised they had talked through take-off and the plane had reached cruising altitude. Their flight attendant brought them another drink and they kept talking.

* * * *

Stepping off the plane four hours later, Tony noticed a group of people with disapproving frowns. Derek squeezed his shoulder.

"Where the hell have you been?" An older man walked up to them, glaring at Tony as he took hold of Derek's arm.

"I took a different flight." Derek shook off the man's hand and turned to face Tony. "Thanks for making it an interesting ride. I'll be watching for you when your circuit starts up again."

Tony ignored the man who must have been Derek's manager and hugged the singer. "I hope you find some happiness somewhere," he whispered in the man's ear.

Derek pulled his sunglasses down so his blue eyes met Tony's. "Someday I will. It just depends on how much more shit I can take. Thanks."

Derek kissed his cheek and Tony didn't say anything else.

Chapter Three

Hardin Ranch, Wyoming, a day later

Tony sat, staring out of his truck window at the rental car in Les' driveway. He knew it was Luis'. He wasn't sure how he felt about seeing his first love again.

The anger he'd felt when he'd received his sister's wedding invitation had disappeared over the years. He'd always known Luis would never come out of the closet. Luis enjoyed his comfortable niche too much.

Les and Randy came out onto the porch and Tony focused on them. Les' arm was around Randy's waist and the younger man rested on him. Tony realised even if he didn't know they were a couple, and if they never touched in public, he would still be able to tell they were together. It was as if an invisible string bound them together.

Luis stood behind them, a sneer on his face. Tony took a deep breath. The years hadn't been kind to his brother-in-law. Too much easy living and good food had given him a bit of a paunch. The black curls, which Tony had loved running his fingers through, were thinning.

He climbed out of his truck before reaching in the back to pull out his equipment bag and luggage. He knew his friends wouldn't stop him if he chose to climb back in and drive away.

Face your past. It's the only way to let go. A voice sounding remarkably like Les' rang in his head.

"I'm back." He smiled up at his friends.

"Good." Randy bolted down the steps and wrapped him in a tight hug. "We missed you."

Les followed more cautiously. But the strength of his hug was the same. "I'm glad you're safe." Les' lips pressed against his ears. "Get him the hell out of my house."

Surprised, Tony jerked back and shot Les a questioning look. Les' dark brown eyes held restrained anger. Tony wondered what Luis had done to cause such a reaction in Les. Les was usually a gracious host—the man didn't have problems opening his home to strangers.

"I will," he murmured.

Les' smile was tight, but he backed away, not saying anything else.

Luis pushed past Randy and Les to hug Tony. Tony struggled against the unexpected embrace.

"Tony, it's been too long. You're looking good, man." Luis held him at arm's length.

His brother-in-law's gaze undressed him and made his skin crawl. Of all the emotions Tony thought he would have felt, revulsion wasn't one of them.

"What are you doing here?" He climbed the steps to stand on the porch.

Randy and Les picked up his bags, taking them into the house for him. Each squeezed his shoulder as they went past.

"What? No 'how are you'? No hello kiss?" Luis ran a finger over Tony's cheek. "It's been a while since I tasted those sweet lips of yours."

"You're married to my sister and you're not gay."

Being hit on was the last thing he'd expected. He felt off-kilter.

His brother-in-law laughed. "It's not like I'm cheating on her."

"You don't consider kissing another guy cheating?"

"Hell, no. I'm not gay, but fags love me. I don't want to disappoint them. Some of the best blow jobs I've gotten were from rent boys in Austin." Luis moved closer.

Tony found himself pinned against the rail of the porch. Luis crushed their lips together. At one time, Tony's favourite thing had been a kiss from this man, but that had been before Luis had broken his heart and turned on him. With a shove, he pushed Luis back, slamming the man into the wall. Tony scrubbed his sleeve over his mouth.

"What the fuck are you doing?" He glared at Luis.

"Come on, Tony. You know you want a piece of me. You were always eager when we were younger. You liked my cock even more than your sister does now."

Tony's brain shut down and his fist flew. Blood exploded from Luis' nose and lip. Luis hunched over, cupping his hand over his injured face.

"Don't ever talk about my sister that way. You're an asshole, Martinez. I don't want you touching or even talking to me. If you do, I'll kick your fucking ass. I'm not the same boy who thought you hung the moon." His hands shook.

Les stepped out, moving to stand beside Tony. "Mr Martinez, you have overstayed your welcome. I suggest you leave now. I'm sure you'll be able to find a hotel in Cheyenne."

Randy tossed Luis' suitcase out on the grass. Luis walked down to grab it, snarling at them with blood dripping from his lip.

"Maria wants you to come and talk to Juan. She's afraid the boy's a queer, just like his uncle. She wrote you and when she didn't hear from you, she sent me. For some reason, they seem to think you can talk some sense into the boy about the dangers of being a fag."

Tony kept his emotions under tight control as Luis snatched his suitcase off the ground and stalked to the car. Silence reigned as Luis raced away from the ranch.

"Good riddance. The man has been driving us crazy since he got here." Randy took Tony's hand and led him into the house, heading for the living room.

"Why didn't you tell us your brother-in-law was so far in the closet he thinks he's straight?" Les stalked towards the kitchen.

Tony allowed Randy to push him down on the couch. He was stunned by Luis' actions. He still hadn't figured out what sort of advice he could give the kid. If Juan really was gay, Tony wasn't about to tell him to deny it.

"Here." Les handed him a shot of whisky.

"A little early to be hitting the bottle," he commented, but drained the glass.

"Thought you'd want to get his taste out of your mouth." Les sat on the arm of the sofa, his hand resting on Randy's shoulder.

"You're right." Tony laughed softly. "It's weird. For months after I ran away, I used to dream of kissing him. The moment *Tía* Elena said he was marrying Angelina, I stopped thinking of him at all, except as a reminder of why I never wanted to go home."

"I can't imagine what it felt like to realise your ex-boyfriend married your sister." Randy's hand ran over Tony's back.

"Looking back on it, I wouldn't consider him a boyfriend, even though I thought he was at the time. He let me suck his dick. That's all. Plus a few kisses once in a while as a treat for me." Tony shuddered. "He's been cheating on her since they started dating, but I can't tell her. She wouldn't believe me and he could paint me as a jealous man who wants him and is willing to break up a marriage to get him." Tony jumped to his feet and started pacing.

"Who are Juan and Maria?" Randy enquired.

"Maria's my oldest sister. Juan's her son and should be around sixteen now."

"Why did they send Luis to talk to you?" Les caressed Randy's neck.

"Maria's husband died last year, so I guess Luis had taken over that role for Juan. My father hasn't spoken to me since I left. Poor Juan. I can't imagine what he's gone through having to deal with Luis and the rest of the family. Especially if he is gay."

"What are you going to do?" Les asked.

Tony gave Les a rueful smile. "I guess I'm going home. I'll have to call *Tía* Elena and see if I can stay with her."

"We'll come with you if you need us," Randy offered.

"Thanks, cowboy, but having me back will be enough of a shock. I don't want to kill them by hauling you two with me." Tony hugged his friend.

"When are you going?"

Les was a master of organisation and Tony was more than willing to allow him to take over planning the trip. He could see the fear and worry in his friends' eyes. They didn't think going back was a good idea.

"Not until after Thanksgiving. I'm not ruining my holiday because of them."

Les hugged him this time. "Great. I want my family here. On Friday, we'll make plans. You can use my plane."

Tony nodded, tears welling in his eyes. Les had welcomed Tony into his home and life with open arms. The man never held anything back if he thought it was needed.

"Show me the new horses and rough stock you guys got while I was away." He needed to think about other things for a while. He winked at Randy. "I'll tell you all about the guy I met in Hawaii."

* * * *

Later that night, he called his aunt. He hoped she hadn't gone to any of his cousins' houses yet for the holiday weekend.

"*Bueno?*"

"*Hola, Tía* Elena. *Es Antonio.*" He wasn't sure what her reaction would be. He hadn't talked to her in several months.

Tía Elena had married his *Tío* Manuel shortly after Tony had run away. They had never met face-to-face, but for some reason, she'd reached out to him and tried to keep in touch.

"Tony. It's wonderful to hear from you. Everything is okay?" *Tía* Elena's voice held a smile.

He relaxed. "*Sí.* I'm fine, but I need to ask a favour."

"Anything. We're family."

"I wish more of them felt that way, *Tía*." He moved out onto the patio off his room.

"There are more of us than you think, but I've honoured your wishes and never told them where you were. I just mailed the letter for them."

"Then how did Luis know where to find me?"

"Luis? Did he visit you, Antonio? I told them to leave you alone and let you make up your mind about coming." Elena sounded angry.

"Yeah. He showed up at the ranch a few days ago, but I wasn't there. He said Maria sent him to get me to come to Austin." Tony felt his anger start to flare again.

"Hmm...I'll have to talk to Maria and see what she has to say." Elena changed the subject. "So, what favour would you ask?"

Tony smiled at her brisk question. "I'm coming to town and I need a place to stay."

"*Cuándo vienes?*"

"I plan on coming down next Monday." Just the thought of returning made him sick to his stomach.

"Ah. I won't be home. I'm going to Dallas for several weeks to visit *mija*. She has a new *niño*." Her excitement bubbled over the phone.

"Congratulations. Don't worry. I'll get a hotel room." Disappointment raced through him, though staying at a hotel would make avoiding family easier.

"No, *mi sobrino*. You must stay at my house," she insisted. "It will make me happy to know it's not empty the entire time I'm gone."

He agreed, feeling an odd burst of happiness knowing she wanted him to use her home.

Chapter Four

Tuesday afternoon

Tony stared out of the window as he drove to his sister's house. The houses on the street were older, but it didn't look like anything else had changed since the last time he'd been there. He looked away as he drove past his parents' house. He wasn't going to stop by and visit them. Didn't need to have the door slammed in his face. He stepped out of the car.

He stood on the sidewalk, trying to gather his courage. Tony had never thought he'd be afraid to see his sister. He was older and had learnt how to survive without approval from his family. Taking a deep breath, he made his way up the walk to the front porch. He knocked on the door and waited.

"Antonio," his sister greeted him coolly.

"Maria. It's nice to see you." He didn't try to enter the house.

"I can see your family means so much to you that it's taken you a week to come." She crossed her arms and glared at him.

"No one is dying and I wished to spend Thanksgiving with family." There wasn't any way he would apologise.

"Ah, yes. Luis told me about those two *gringos* you live with. Are they your boyfriends, Antonio?" Her disgust and scorn dripped like venom in her words.

"Stop right there, Maria Mendoza. I haven't come here to let you pass judgement on my friends or me. I didn't come for you. I'd be more than happy to go back to Wyoming and forget I ever had family in Texas."

No guilt. It had taken three years after he had run away before he'd stopped feeling guilty because he was gay. He wouldn't allow his sister to take him back into his old ways.

"Mama, who's this?"

Tony turned to see a tall, good-looking teenager standing at the bottom of the porch steps. His heart skipped a beat. If this was Juan and he was gay, the boy would have to beat the men off with a stick when he was older.

"You must be Juan. I'm your *Tío* Antonio." Tony held out his hand. He wasn't sure what Maria might have told his nephew about him, so he didn't expect Juan to actually shake his hand.

"*Tío* Tony?" A bright smile broke over the young man's face. Juan bounded up the steps, ignored Tony's hand and hugged him. "*Tía* Elena said you were coming for a visit. Are you staying at her place?"

"Yes. At least for a little while." Tony hugged his nephew.

"Juan, go inside and do your homework." Maria's voice was frigid now.

"But I want to talk to *Tío* Tony," Juan protested.

"Maybe later. I'll be here for a week or so." Tony clapped the boy's shoulder.

"Great." Juan smiled. The teenager kissed his mother's cheek as he went by her.

Tony waited until his nephew was out of hearing range. "Do you want me to talk to him or not?"

"I'm not sure it'd be a good idea to let you into his life. Juan's a good boy, Antonio. I don't want you influencing him."

"You mean seducing him to the dark side. Don't worry about that, sis. I wouldn't dream of corrupting him." Tony turned to leave, but something made him stop and look back at Maria. "Please, promise me, you'll love him no matter what. Don't make him have to choose between you and his happiness."

Maria shut the door in his face. Tony sighed and headed towards the rental car. Why had he come home? He'd known it was a stupid thing to do, yet deep inside, he'd hoped things had changed. Judging by his sister's attitude, they hadn't changed at all.

"*Tío* Tony."

Looking up, he saw Juan standing beside his car. He glanced back to see if Maria could see them.

"Don't worry. She's on the phone, arguing with *Tía* Angelina." Juan shifted nervously.

"Won't she be angry with you for talking to me?" Tony didn't want to get Juan in trouble with his mom.

"I'll be back inside before they're done. Can we talk?"

"That's what I'm here for. Come see me at *Tía* Elena's." Tony rummaged around his rental car, finding a piece of paper and a pen. He scribbled down his cell number. "Call me before you come over."

"*Muchas gracias, Tío* Tony." Juan tucked the paper in his pocket. "*Tía* Elena said I should talk to you."

"Yeah, well, I'll be glad to help, but I don't want to cause problems for you. As you can see, I'm not very popular around here." Tony gestured at the houses surrounding them.

His nephew shrugged. "There were problems before you came. I should go. I'll call you tomorrow."

He watched Juan jog back to the house. His nephew's tone told him things weren't perfect in paradise. He'd have to wait until tomorrow to find out why.

* * * *

Later that night, Tony settled on his aunt's couch with a beer and the remote. He'd just flipped on a basketball game when his cell phone rang. Toby Keith's '*Should've Been a Cowboy*' blared out.

"Hey there, Les." He grinned as he leant back against the cushions.

"Tony. How's old home week going?" Les' drawl held laughter.

"Why didn't you tie me up and refuse to let me come down here?" He scrubbed a hand over his face. "I don't know why I thought this would be a good idea."

"Because if what your ass of a brother-in-law says is right, you don't want your nephew going through the same crap you did."

Les was right. Tony didn't want to risk Juan feeling that the entire world hated him, like Tony had.

"You're right as usual. Doesn't Randy ever get tired of your perfection?" he teased.

Les chuckled. "Randy loves me, so he's blind to my faults. You better not try to open his eyes to them, either."

"I wouldn't want to disillusion the kid. Couldn't stand to see him disappointed."

"We agree on that." Les' words held a fond tone.

A voice spoke in the background.

Les' voice was muffled then he came back on to tell Tony, "Peter needs me to sign some checks. I'll have Randy call you tomorrow evening."

"Great. I'll need to hear the voice of reason by then."

"Well, then I'll have Margie call. She's the only reasonable voice we have on the ranch."

Tony was still laughing when he tossed the phone on the end table. Talking to Les eased him. Maybe it was because he didn't have to hide his true nature. He didn't have to be anyone other than Tony with Les.

* * * *

By three the next day, Tony was bored. He'd fixed all the little problems *Tía* Elena had needed to be done. His cousin, Marcus, lived in New York and didn't get home often. *Tía* Elena probably didn't want to bother anyone, so more than likely she never complained. Tony had decided to help her out as payment for letting him stay at her place.

Pacing through the living room, he tried to think of something to do. If he'd been at the ranch, he'd have been helping with the rough stock, working some of the cutting horses, or just out riding the fence line. In town, there wasn't anything to do and he didn't have any friends there to hang out with.

When his phone rang, a sense of relief hit him. Finally, something was happening.

"Yeah?" He threw himself into a recliner.

"*Tío* Tony? It's Juan. I was wondering if I could come over and talk with you." Juan's voice held a hint of hesitation.

"Sure. Come on over." Tony didn't have a clue what to say to the boy, but he'd try.

"Cool. I'm only a few minutes away." Juan hung up.

Tony set his phone down and headed for the kitchen. When he was Juan's age, he'd been hungry all the time, and not just from being homeless. After opening the fridge, he pulled out stuff to make sandwiches.

True to his word, Juan walked in the back door a few minutes later. The teenager dropped his backpack on a counter and grabbed a soda along with a sandwich.

"What'd you tell your mom? Seems like she changed her mind about me talking to you." Tony leaned against the sink and watched Juan inhale the food.

"I'm not sure what she wanted you to do for me, but yes, she took one look at you and decided she didn't want you anywhere near me. Told her I was going to a friend's house to study and I'd eat there." Juan took a bite from his second sandwich. "Hey, man, these aren't bad."

"When you've been on your own for as long as I have, you learn a thing or two. Though I do thank my lucky stars I hooked up with Les and Randy. Les' housekeeper, Margie, is a cook to die for." He grinned, thinking about Les' feisty housekeeper.

"Wow. A housekeeper? He must have money." Juan's eyes widened.

"Yeah, he does, but Margie's been with him so long she's part of the family." He hooked a chair leg and pulled it over to him. After flipping it around, he straddled the seat to rest his arms across the back. "So talk."

Juan's cheeks flushed and the teenager ducked his head. "How did you know?"

"Know what?" Tony wasn't going to make it easy for his nephew.

"That you were...you know—" Juan gestured to Tony.

"Was what? Come on, kiddo. I can't help you if you won't even say the word." He reached out and lifted Juan's chin, forcing the young man to meet his gaze. "Look me in the eye when you say it."

Juan took a deep breath. "How'd you know you were gay?"

"Good boy." Tony smiled. "I was never interested in girls, except to play with. By the time I was fifteen, I understood my preferences didn't follow normal social lines."

"When did you kiss a boy for the first time?" Juan sat forward, eager to listen.

"I was fifteen. He was popular and everything I thought I wanted, but he was just using me while his girlfriend was gone for the summer." Tony wasn't going to mention any names.

"Was the guy the reason you told your parents?"

Tony nodded. "I was an idiot. I thought by telling them, we wouldn't have to hide anymore. Little did I know he just wanted me to blow him." He'd already decided not to talk down to Juan or treat the teenager like an innocent virgin. That wouldn't help the young man make the right decision.

"What did you do?"

"I tried to ignore the comments and the snubs from the neighbours. I didn't understand why it was any of their business. Then one day some boy's dad came to talk to my father. He told Papa I'd tried to seduce his son. I denied it. I hadn't touched anyone since I'd told my parents. My father looked right through me and said he didn't have a son, only daughters." The pain ripped through Tony as if he were hearing those words for the first time.

"Shit. I can't believe *Abuelo* would say that." Juan shook his head.

Understanding why Juan would defend his grandpa still didn't make Tony feel better. "If you're gay, Juan, and choose to come out, I can guarantee your *abuelo* will disown you. He's very traditional. I haven't talked to him since I left."

"I'm gay, *Tío* Tony. I've known for a while now. I just haven't been able to work up the courage to tell my mother. I'm not sure exactly how she worked it out." Juan picked at the crust of one leftover sandwich.

"Do you have a boyfriend?" He didn't see how that would be possible without anyone finding out.

"No, but I have a few friends who know. Some weekends, we go to the clubs in Austin."

"You're only sixteen." Tony glared at Juan.

"I have a fake ID. It says I'm eighteen. I don't drink. We go to dance with other guys like us. Makes us feel less lonely." Juan smiled.

Tony didn't yell. He knew how isolated being gay had made him and he might have done the same thing, if the option had been open to him.

"You're safe, right? Don't leave with strangers. Never accept drinks from anyone. Condoms?" Juan was a teenage boy. Tony wasn't going to hide his head in the sand about his nephew having sex.

"Well, I haven't done anything but kiss. I'm not ready for it and I definitely don't want it to be with some guy I picked up at the club." Juan blushed. "Is it too girly to say I'd like it to mean something? I don't want to look back at my first time and be embarrassed by it."

"Not girly at all, Juan. Pretty smart actually. People like to think differently, but having sex for the first time is important to guys as well. Though there are a bunch of macho men who'd like you to think otherwise." He grabbed a beer and another soda from the fridge then handed the can to Juan. "You've never talked to anyone about this?"

"Only *Tía* Elena. I keep my club clothes here. She covers for me when we go dancing. She's the one who suggested I talk to you. I was planning on calling you the day you showed up on our doorstep." Juan popped the top and took a swig.

"I've never understood why she goes out of her way to keep in touch with me. I know *Tío* Manuel didn't want anything to do with me." He frowned.

"She's never really explained. The only thing she's said to me is that family sticks together, no matter what." His nephew glanced at him. "She figured if you knew one person still cared about you, you wouldn't get into too much trouble."

It made sense in an odd sort of way. Tony vowed to buy *Tía* Elena a thank-you present. She needed to know how much he appreciated everything she'd done for him.

Tony rejoined Juan at the table. "So, what else did you want to know?"

Juan flashed a bright grin. "Everything."

* * * *

Two hours later, Juan's cell phone rang, interrupting their conversation.

"Hey, Mom." Juan rolled his eyes.

Tony smiled, glancing at the clock on the wall. No wonder Maria was calling to find out where her son was.

"Yeah. I'm heading home in a minute." A frown chased across Juan's face.

Tony waited until Juan had hung up and had grabbed his backpack before he said, "You're not in trouble, are you?"

Juan shot him a look. "*Tío* Luis and *Tía* Angelina are visiting and Mom wants me home."

An emotion showed in his nephew's dark eyes for a second but it was gone before Tony could identify it.

"Thanks for talking to me. It's nice to have someone who's gone through the same thing as me, and who understands the family." Juan gave Tony a quick hug.

"Anytime. You have my phone number—call. I'll help you all I can."

Tony watched the young man walk away. He hoped he'd helped Juan figure things out, but he wasn't sure where that would lead his nephew next.

* * * *

Randy rolled over, reaching across Les' body to grab the phone. "Hello," he mumbled.

"Hey, handsome. When you going to dump Les and run away with me?" Tony's voice slurred over the phone.

Randy pushed himself up so he could rest against the headboard. He stroked Les' head. "Tony?"

"Who else would it be? Do a lot of guys ask you to run away with them?" Tony chuckled.

"Strangely enough, you're the only one."

Tony was drunk and Randy wasn't happy about that, since he was already worried about Tony being down in Austin surrounded by people who hated him. Randy should've gone with him as backup.

"Always was a stubborn ass. Have you ever wondered if being gay's hereditary?"

Tony was the only person Randy knew whose vocabulary actually got better when the man was drunk.

"No. I haven't. I'm not a deep thinker like you and Les."

Les stared up at him and he mouthed, 'Tony'. His lover nodded and snuggled against his hip.

"Shit, man. I'm not deep. I'm as shallow as a mud puddle. Your life partner? He's deep. It's like conversing with fucking Gandhi, talking to Les sometimes." A crash sounded in the background.

"Are you all right?" Randy's concern grew.

"Sure am. Tripped over a few bottles." Tony grunted.

"When did you start drinking, Tony?" He tried to remember the last time Tony'd been this drunk.

"Let's see. Juan left about five. I went to the store and got snubbed by my father. That had to have been around six. So I'd say I started at seven. What time is it now?"

Randy checked the clock. "It's midnight."

"Five hours. Beer and whisky. I'm going to be sicker than a dog tomorrow, aren't I?" Tony asked.

"Yes, I think you will, babe," Randy agreed. "So you talked to your nephew?"

"Yep. He's queer too. It must run in the family, though I'd never tell that to my father. Probably give the man a coronary." Tony sighed. "Thing is, Randy, the kid's got things figured out already. Don't know what good talking to me did him. I should have sent Les to chat with him. He could have explained things better."

"Les can be helpful, but Juan wouldn't have talked to him. First of all, Les is a *gringo* and you all tend to be tight-lipped around us. Second, Les' experiences aren't the same as ours. His father loved him and accepted him. You know how Juan's mother's going to react because it's how your parents reacted. You're the best one for your nephew to talk to, Tony." Randy wanted to reach through the phone and wrap his arms around his friend, right after he slapped Tony silly for getting drunk.

"I'm lonely, cowboy."

Tony's admission was so low, Randy almost didn't hear it. The words and tone cut Randy's heart. He squeezed Les' shoulder. Les frowned and sat up, putting his ear next to the phone.

"I know you are. It's hard to be in a place where no one seems to care or even want you." Randy entangled his fingers with Les'.

"Not just here. I expected that. No one's ever cared for me here. I want what you have with Les. Sometimes it hurts to see you two together." Tony's voice faded then Randy heard his friend mutter, "I miss Mac. Stupid, isn't it? I've had one-night stands before and none of them made me dream of them a week after I slept with them. I can't stop thinking about him."

Randy glanced at Les. Surprise and sadness welled in his lover's eyes. They had never meant to hurt Tony.

"God. I'm being a girl. Now I know why I don't get drunk very often. Ignore me. Go back to bed, cowboy, and forget I ever said anything." Tony hung up.

Randy dropped the receiver back on its base. Les wrapped his arms around Randy's waist and they held each other tight.

"We won't mention this conversation unless Tony brings it up," Les said.

Randy nodded. He wouldn't forget it, but he didn't want his friend to be embarrassed.

"If he's not home by Friday, I'm going to get him." Randy didn't want Tony staying anyway any longer.

"I'll go with you." Les kissed the frown from Randy's lips.

Chapter Five

Thursday

Tony walked up the block towards his sister's house. He'd had another talk with Juan and had come to the conclusion his nephew had a pretty good head on his shoulders. Whatever decision the boy made, Juan would think it through first.

His cell rang just as he heard a scream come from Maria's house. He started jogging and answered his phone.

"Hello?"

"*Tío* Tony, can you come over?" Juan sounded upset.

"Actually, I'm right outside your house." He flipped his phone shut and raced up the steps.

Maria was shrieking. "Get this *puto* out of my house." Her hands were waving and slashing towards a young man on the porch.

Juan stood, protecting the older boy from Maria. His own face bore a red handprint.

"What's going on here?" Tony demanded.

Maria whirled on him. "I should've known you coming home would bring evil in your wake. This is your fault. My Juan was a good boy until you came. Now he's bringing home *putos* like him."

"A whore? Why would Juan bring home a rent boy?" Tony was puzzled.

He glanced at the boy Juan stood in front of. He looked to be eighteen and was dressed in skin-tight jeans and T-shirt. Under the bruises, the young man was beautiful. The kind who would be able to make good money selling his body. Tony frowned. There was something familiar about those clear blue eyes.

"Yancey needs a place to stay, Mama. I told him he could stay with us." Juan held his hands out to plead with his mother.

"Your *Tío* Luis warned me that *putos* like him would try to seduce my innocent boy. I should have kept a closer watch on you." Maria's eyes filled with tears.

"Stop it. Take a deep breath, Maria. There's a simple solution. Yancey, you can stay with me at *Tía* Elena's." Tony looked at his sister. "How does Luis know about rent boys?"

Maria swung, catching Tony hard on the cheek with the flat of her hand. "You won't speak ill of Luis. He and Angelina have been good to me since Diego died. Luis is trying to be a father to Juan." She swung again.

Tony caught her wrist and held it tight. "Don't ever hit me again. I'm not your son. I know exactly what Luis is. Yancey, start heading down the street." Tony let go of Maria's hand. He ignored her sputtering and looked at Juan. "If you need me, you know where to find me. I'm leaving tomorrow morning."

Yancey had managed to get to the bottom of the steps by the time Tony reached him. He could see the younger man was sore. He cupped Yancey's elbow to give him a little more support. Yancey looked behind them and Tony turned to see Maria slap Juan again. His grip tightened until Yancey grunted.

"Sorry," he muttered.

Yancey shrugged. "What's one more bruise?"

"Tony, Yancey. Wait." Juan raced down the stairs towards them.

Maria screamed from the porch. "If you go with them, Juan, you're no longer my son."

Tony saw Juan flinch, but his stride didn't falter.

"You don't want to do this, man. She's mad but if you go back, she'll forgive you." Yancey tried to reason with Juan.

Tony unlocked the car doors. He opened one to let Yancey sit.

"I'm going with you." The stubborn set of Juan's chin spoke of his determination.

Yancey turned to glare at Tony. "You're his uncle, man. Why aren't you trying to send him back?"

Tony glanced from the two young men to where his sister still stood, screeching, on the steps. "I ran away from this family. Sue me because I think Juan's better off without them."

"She's his mother." Confusion shone in Yancey's blue eyes.

"Some mothers aren't the angels they're supposed to be." Tony nodded to the car. "Get in."

* * * *

Juan fell asleep after crying in Tony's arms. He tucked his nephew into *Tía* Elena's guest bed then stood, staring down at the teenager. *This is what it feels like to be a parent.*

A noise from the hallway caught his attention. He stepped out to find Yancey standing there, a frown on his bruised face.

"Why?" the bleached-blond teenager asked.

"Come on into the living room. We don't want to wake him. He needs his rest for school tomorrow." Tony led the way, gesturing for Yancey to sit on the couch while he flung his tired body in a chair.

Yancey sat slowly, wincing as his sore muscles protested. The young man was dressed in a pair of Tony's sweats and a loose T-shirt. Even through the bruises and creases of pain alongside of Yancey's mouth, his blue eyes were jarring something in Tony.

"You look like I feel after getting the shit stomped out of me by a bull. What got you?"

"I was in the wrong place at the wrong time. Got in the middle of a gang fight. I ended up in the hospital overnight, but I don't have any insurance, so I couldn't afford to stay any longer." Yancey wrapped an arm around his waist, protecting his ribs.

Tony got up and went to where his bags were sitting by the front door. He dug out a bottle of aspirin. After getting Yancey a glass of water, he held out two pills.

"Thanks." Yancey swallowed them and curled up on the couch. "Why are you doing this?"

"Doing what? Giving you a place to stay?" Tony sat down again. "Not forcing Juan to go back home?"

"Yes."

"Sometimes the family you've got isn't the one you need. It took me eight years to find the one for me and I don't want Juan to have to go searching as well." He studied the hustler. "As for you. You look like a good kid. Maybe you haven't made the greatest of choices, but you made the best of what was available at the time. I've been on the streets and pure dumb luck was all that saved me from doing what you've been doing. I think with a different set of options, you'll make better choices."

"You don't look down on me because I sell myself?" Yancey yawned.

"Nope. I try not to judge people. None of us are perfect. I've learnt that." Tony watched the young man's eyes drift shut. "Who's to say you have to keep doing it?"

Yancey's answer was a soft snore. Tony tugged the blanket off the back of the couch and covered the kid. He went to the kitchen, grabbed a beer from the fridge and went outside. He relished the harsh burn of smoke in his lungs when he lit his cigarette.

He was thinking about turning in when Randy called.

"You ready to come home?" Randy's voice washed over him.

"I'm packed and ready, cowboy. It's been a fucked-up day." He took a drag and blew the smoke out in a sigh.

"What happened now?" Randy's concerned question was a balm to Tony's soul.

Tony told him. After explaining, he concluded by saying, "Now I have a black-and-blue hustler on my couch and an emotionally wounded teenager in the guest room. I have no idea how Yancey and Juan know each other. I'm guessing it must be from the clubs."

"Shit. Would your sister really throw Juan out?" Randy sounded upset.

"With Luis and Angelina encouraging her, I'd say yes. I'm hoping she'll think about it tonight and realise what she's throwing away."

"God, I thought my family was screwed up." Randy laughed.

"Every family's fucked up. It's a law or something." He put out his smoke. "I'll be back at the ranch tomorrow night, but I might be bringing someone with me."

"That's fine. We have the room." Randy didn't hesitate.

Tony had known what Randy and Les' response would be. They never turned anyone away if they could help them instead.

"Thanks. I'll give you a call when we're about to leave here. Can someone pick us up at the airport?"

"We'll be there. Get some sleep." Randy hung up.

Tony lit another cigarette and sat down on the porch steps. He thought about Randy and Les wrapped up in each other's arms, oblivious to the world around them. He thought how happy it made him to see his friends so in love with each other, and how lonely it made him feel. Resting his head against the railing, he closed his eyes. His mind slipped back to the last night in Hawaii.

The rough touch of Mac's hands on his skin, sweat sealing their bodies together as they made love in his condo, the moonlight turning Mac's blond hair silver.

Pressure built behind Tony's eyes. A tear leaked from one corner to trail down his cheek. God, it was stupid to miss someone as much as he'd come to miss Mac. How was it possible a man he'd only known for one night had come to mean so much to him?

He wanted to call Randy back and ask if this aching in his chest was how Randy felt every time he spent time away from Les. He chuckled. Randy had urged him to try to find Mac. Now that he was heading back to Wyoming, he wished he'd listened to his friend and hunted Mac down. Maybe he could have convinced the man to meet him at the ranch. Maybe he could have driven the loneliness away.

Snuffing out the cigarette, he stared up at the stars gleaming in the night sky. Wishing had never got him anything. He needed to forget. He had another month before the PBR events started again—he'd find a way.

* * * *

Randy searched the crowd, looking for Tony. Les stood behind him with an indulgent smile.

"Where is he?"

"You'd think Tony was your boyfriend the way you're carrying on," Les teased.

A rueful expression appeared on Randy's face. "I'm sorry, love," he said softly.

"Don't be. I know you're excited to have him back. Tony's our friend, baby, and he went to a place where he'd be alone, surrounded by people who've already hurt him once. When you care for someone, you want to protect them." Les squeezed Randy's shoulder. "He's here."

Randy turned to see their friend making his way towards them. He studied Tony's dark eyes. Exhaustion and sadness swirled in them. He ignored the stares of the people closest to them and flung his arms around Tony's muscular body, hugging the man tight.

All the tension left the body in his arms and Randy heard Tony sigh.

Tony stepped back, waving to a young man standing a few feet away. "Randy and Les, meet Yancey. He's had a hard time of it lately. I thought we could put him to work on the ranch 'til he got straightened out."

Les shook Yancey's hand. "You're welcome to stay as long as you want." Les hugged Tony then gestured for Yancey to follow him. "We'll go get the car."

Yancey gave Tony a quick glance. Tony nodded. Randy watched them walk away.

"Who is he?"

"His name's Yancey MacCafferty. He's been hustling for a year or two. He got caught in a gang fight a couple of days ago and Juan brought him to my sister's house. Maria had a meltdown. She threw Juan out." Tony rubbed his forehead.

"So where's Juan?" Randy guided Tony to the luggage claim.

"I made him stay at *Tía* Elena's. Maybe with both of us out of the picture, Maria will take him back." Tony shrugged. "Maybe she won't. Juan's not going to hide anymore and I'm afraid she won't take it."

"We'll cross that bridge when it comes." Randy wanted Tony to forget things for a while. "Let's get to the ranch. You can hang out with us, ride some bulls and get ready for next year. Christmas is just around the corner, too. We're having all the rest of the family in for two weeks."

Tony smiled, but Randy had the oddest feeling his friend was tired in his soul and Randy didn't know how to fix that.

Chapter Six

Two weeks later

Brody MacCafferty checked the address he'd jotted down. He studied the house in front of him. It was a small ranch-style home with a white porch on the front.

He sighed. It'd taken him a month to untangle the trail his brother had left when the idiot had run away from his aunt's house in Dallas. Now it was time to get his brother's ass back home. He climbed the steps and knocked.

A tiny Hispanic woman opened the door. "*Sí?*"

"Hello, are you Mrs Elena Romanos?"

"*Sí.*" The woman smiled.

"I was told you might be able to help me find my brother."

"*Tía* Elena?" A young man came down the hall, a soda in his hand. "Who's at the door?"

"A *gringo* looking for his *hermano.*" Mrs Romanos opened the door wider. "He says I might know where he is."

"Brother?" The kid got closer. When he saw Brody, his eyes widened. "Shit, you look just like him."

"Juan, language." She waved Brody in. "Come in and sit. Would you like a soda?"

"Yes, please." As eager as he was to find out what Juan knew, he didn't want to insult Mrs Romanos.

"*Bueno*. Juan, take our guest to the living room and tell him about his *hermano*."

"*Sí, Tía* Elena. Will you come with me, Mr MacCafferty?" Juan led the way and gestured for Brody to choose a seat.

"Call me Brody. How did you meet Yancey?" He knew what Yancey had been doing before he had disappeared, but Juan didn't look like the kind of kid who hustled. He gave himself a mental shake. Yancey hadn't seemed like the type either.

"We met at some clubs in Austin." Juan curled up in a chair across from the couch Brody sat on.

"You don't look old enough."

Mrs Romanos brought his drink to him. He smiled and thanked her.

"Fake ID. Never tried to order a drink, so they didn't check too close. Yancey sort of took me under his wing. Made sure I knew which guys were there to dance and which ones were looking for more. He taught me how to send out the right signals. The ones that weren't going to get me trouble. We became friends." Juan grinned. "You look so much like him. Now I know how hot he'll be when he's your age." The kid blushed.

"Thanks. Do you know where he is?" Brody's voice shook in his excitement. He was getting closer.

"Sure. I talked to him last night. After he got out of the hospital, he needed a place to stay."

Fear shot through Brody. "Hospital? What happened?"

"I'm not sure. He just said he got caught in a gang fight. Got beat up. He's fine now. My *Tío* said Yancey needed time to straighten things out." Juan stared at him, searching for something.

"Where is he?"

"You know, I asked him once about his family. He said his dad could barely take care of himself and his brother had to leave town because of some bad shit he got involved in." Juan's gaze dropped to the can he held in his hand. "Why now?"

Brody gave the kid credit. Juan wasn't going to give him information until he was satisfied with Brody's answers.

"I got tired of running. Five years ago, I ran away from a dangerous situation I created for myself. Once I got away from here, I started getting back on the right side of the law. I got work as a bodyguard and opened my own business. About two months ago, I met someone who left an impression on me. He made me realise family is the most important thing and I managed to throw mine away. So I decided it was time to come and round them up, repair some bridges and form new bonds." Brody thought of Tony. "My dad's got his life straightened out on his own, but I need to find Yancey."

"I thought someone would come looking for Yancey." Mrs Romanos held out a piece of paper.

Brody took the paper, glancing between Juan and the lady. "What does this have to do with my brother?"

"He's in Wyoming with my *tío*. He's helping out on the ranch of a friend of my *tío's*. Call him. You'll be able to talk to Yancey as well." Juan stood, his brown eyes sad as he looked at his aunt. "Mama wouldn't talk to me. I tried, but I'm done beating my head against a wall. I talked to *Tío* Tony. He's going to try to discuss with Mama about me living with him."

"Maria always was a stubborn girl. It's for the best, *mijo*. Your *tío* will take care of you." Elena patted Juan's cheek.

Brody stood as well. "Thank you for the number and the soda."

"You're welcome. Don't disappoint your brother." Mrs Romanos gave him a fierce hug.

"I won't," Brody said. He waved goodbye and left the house.

As excited as he was to finally be close to talking to his brother, he waited until he got to his hotel before calling. He pulled off his shirt and shoes, settling on the bed to dial the number.

"Romanos."

Images of a dark-haired cowboy laughing at him with a wreath of cigarette smoke around his head flashed through his mind. He shook his head. There was no way it could be the same guy. It had to be the accent making him think he knew the man he was talking to.

"I'm looking for Yancey MacCafferty."

"Who's looking?"

The accent still brought images of naked skin to mind, but now the man's voice held an edge.

"His brother." He could play the hardass game too.

"It's about damn time. What took you so fucking long? Shit. I thought he was wrong and you were dead." Romanos didn't sound happy Brody was calling about Yancey.

"Um…" Brody was at a loss. He hadn't expected to get chewed out by a stranger, but there really was something familiar about the voice on the other end of the phone. The man's name was Tony and he lived in Wyoming. He must be a cowboy. Brody shook his head. Nah, too impossible. There had to be a hundred cowboys in Wyoming named Tony. It didn't mean this one was the one he'd spent the night with in Hawaii.

"Hell. I guess it doesn't matter. You're calling now." Romanos faded away for a second. "He's down at the barn working the horses with Randy."

"I had to get other parts of my life taken care of so I could take time off to spend with Yancey when I found him. Thank God, my dad is okay. Yancey'd been gone two years. It took me until last week to figure out where he'd gone." Brody didn't know why he was explaining things to this man.

"Oh. How's your dad doing?" Romanos sounded interested, but there was a hint of scepticism in the man's voice.

"He's gotten his own life back on track. I never thought I'd see the day when he would actually take a day off work and hang out with his son, but he did that the day before I left for Austin." Brody realised he hadn't introduced himself. "My name's…"

"I don't need to know your name." Tony glared out of the window.

He saw Yancey talking to Jackson and lunging one of the younger horses. Welcoming Yancey's older brother with open arms wasn't in Tony's realm of understanding at the moment. He didn't trust that MacCafferty was truly interested in finding Yancey.

"What's going on between you and my brother?" MacCafferty enquired.

"There's nothing going on between us. I saw he needed help, plus it made my nephew happy. Besides, he really is too young for me." Why was he trying to reassure Yancey's brother? It didn't matter if anything was going on between Tony and Yancey. The older brother didn't have any say in the younger man's life.

"We'll see," the man said.

Crazy as it was, excitement laced with his scepticism and wound through Tony at his statement. He didn't know the man from Adam, but something about MacCafferty's voice created a rush of lust in Tony's body.

"I'm sure if you want to see your brother, you'll figure out how to find him."

He wasn't going to make it easy for MacCafferty.

"Thank you for taking Yancey in, Romanos."

"Your brother needed some place to heal."

"I'll talk to you again. Bye." MacCafferty hung up.

Tony set his phone down and stared at it. He adjusted his cock, trying to find room in his jeans. What did that man have to make just talking to him give Tony a hard-on?

"Yancey's brother is coming out?"

He looked up to see Les standing in the doorway.

"So it would seem." He thrust his hand through his hair and shook his head.

Les laughed, coming to him and throwing an arm around his shoulder. "You haven't even met the man and you're already flustered. Do you know his brother?"

"That's the thing. I don't know him, yet talking to him made me hard. It's weird, but when I saw Yancey, the kid looked familiar to me and now his older brother sounds like someone I've met before." Tony frowned.

"Maybe you have. The world is actually much smaller than we think it is. He might have been someone you talked to at an event. I can't wait to meet him. Yancey's such a great kid, for all his issues. I wouldn't be surprised if MacCafferty's just as interesting." Les glanced over as Randy walked in.

"What's going on?" Randy kissed Les' cheek and winked at Tony.

"Just got a phone call from Yancey's older brother. He's looking for the kid. I told him if he wanted to see him, he knew where to find him."

"Why didn't you have him talk to Yancey?" Les frowned.

"I'm not building up that kid's hopes, in case MacCafferty doesn't show up. Yancey's been through a lot of shit. It's been five years since he's had any contact with his brother. What if the jerk decides to head back to wherever he's living now and not come looking for Yancey?" He scrubbed a hand over his face.

"You can't make the decision for him. He wants to see his brother. He talks to me about the man all the time." Randy took Tony's hand. "Try to be open-minded about this whole thing. There are families where the members love each other and want to be together."

He looked down, shuffling his feet like a chastised kid. "You're right."

"Cool. Remember we're taking Lindsay out to San Diego and meeting Rick for a couple of days," Randy pointed out as he went down the hall to the bedrooms.

Les groaned. "I forgot about that. I'm sure he'll still be here when we get back."

"If MacCafferty shows, I'll tell him he can stay as long as he wants. Thanks." Tony grabbed his coat and hat. He was going to head out to the barns and spend some time with the horses. Maybe they'd help him calm down, because he couldn't believe he was nervous about meeting a stranger.

* * * *

Later that night, Tony walked through the kitchen where Yancey was washing dishes for Margie.

"Yancey, would you come outside with me for a minute?" He shrugged into his jacket, patting his pocket to make sure his cigarettes were there.

"Sure. Let me finish up here and I'll be right out." Yancey shot him a smile.

"Fair enough."

He wandered out on the porch. Leaning against the rail, he lit a cigarette. His nerves relaxed as the dull acidic burn filled his lungs.

Ever since Yancey's older brother had called, Tony had been trying to decide if he should tell the kid about the call or not. Part of him said Yancey should be prepared if MacCafferty showed up. Another part said telling Yancey was setting the young man up for disappointment if he didn't show.

God knew Tony had waited long enough for one of his family to come for him. They never did. He couldn't be confident MacCafferty really wanted to find Yancey.

"You wanted to talk to me?"

The door slammed behind Yancey. Tony smiled at the younger man. He shook off the feeling he should be seeing more in Yancey's face, more lines or signs of maturity. Those blue eyes should be a brighter blue.

"We've never talked about how you'd feel if your brother came looking for you."

"You mean when he comes." Yancey's voice held conviction.

"How can you be so sure he'll come looking for you? It's been what? Five years? Don't you think he'd have returned sooner?" He took a drag on his cigarette.

Yancey sat in one of the rocking chairs Les kept on the porch. "I've seen how your family is and I'm not surprised you're a little sceptical." Yancey rocked. "Brody isn't like that. He left because he didn't have a choice."

Tony was about to say everyone had a choice. He caught himself before he said anything. He'd run away because he hadn't thought he'd had one.

"By the time Brody was a senior in high school, he was in some deep shit. Gangs. Drugs." Yancey shrugged. "I'm not sure how long he'd been using, but it got to the point where someone was going to get killed. He left the night he graduated."

He stared up at the clear night sky. Bright stars twinkled in the black velvet dark. "You haven't heard from or seen him in five years."

"I waited for him on the front porch the night he left. He told me as soon as he cleaned up, he'd come back. We stayed in touch for a couple of months before the calls stopped." Yancey sighed. "I figure it's taken him longer to get clean than he planned."

"Five years. Two of which you spent on the street." Tony shook his head and studied the tip of his cigarette. "Why don't you resent him?"

The kid chuckled. "Living on the street was my decision, Tony. I could have stayed at my aunt's, but I thought I could take care of myself. I did a lot of stuff I'm not proud of and I'm lucky I didn't get beaten up or killed."

Tony snubbed out his smoke and sat down on the top step. "I don't understand."

"I know." Yancey spoke softly. "Maybe it's simply because he didn't abandon me. We talked about why he was leaving. I understood. I'd rather he live on the other side of the world without me than live as a druggie."

Maybe MacCafferty was interested in seeing Yancey. Tony would withhold judgement until the man showed up on his front steps.

"He'll come looking for me. I'm not naïve, Tony, but I have faith."

"I hope your faith pays off, Yancey. I really do."

Yancey yawned. "I'm heading to bed. Don't stay out here too much longer. It's freezing."

"'Night, kid, I'm going to have one more smoke and I'll be in."

He lit his last cigarette for the night and closed his eyes. This time his thoughts didn't wander to MacCafferty coming for Yancey. His mind went to a big blond man who'd rocked his world for one night in paradise.

He let his body sink into the heat and lust-filled memories of that night. Maybe he should go out to L.A. and find Mac.

Chapter Seven

Brody stood outside Elena Romanos' house again. This time Juan answered the door. He studied the teenager. The sadness was still there in those brown eyes, plus there was a hint of strength, telling Brody the boy would do what he thought was right, no matter what.

"Can you give me your uncle's address?"

Juan gave him a wavering smile. Those big brown eyes filled with tears. "Are you going to see Yancey?" Juan stepped back to allow him in.

"Yeah, I am." Juan's sadness cut Brody to the quick. Brody tossed an arm around Juan's shoulder and squeezed. "I hope your mother figures out what a great kid she has and how much she'll be missing if she kicks you out."

"I certainly hope so. I have to say *mia sobrina* disappoints me." Elena Romanos came out of the kitchen. She handed Brody a piece of paper. "Here's the address for Hardin Ranch where your *hermano* is staying."

Brody nodded at Mrs Romanos. "It was nice meeting you, Señora Romanos."

"Call me *Tía* Elena, *por favor*. I have a feeling you and your brother will be part of my family." She hugged him.

Juan hugged him tight as well. "I'm glad you're going to see him. No one should be without family."

"I just hope he welcomes me as easily as you have." He turned to leave. "Take care, kid. Things will work out."

* * * *

Several hours later, Brody settled into his seat and took a deep breath.

"You don't like to fly?"

He clenched the armrests and stared in front of him as the plane began to back away from the gate. "Can't say I'm thrilled to be doing this. What the hell are you doing here?"

"My mom threw me out and *Tío* Tony agreed to let me come and stay with him. *Tía* Elena bought me the ticket yesterday." Juan stared back at him.

"Did you know you were going to be on the same flight as me?"

"No. Since I am though, can I catch a ride to the ranch with you?" Juan's dark eyes sparkled at him.

There was that déjà vu feeling again. He swore he'd seen eyes like that smile at him when he woke up that morning in Hawaii.

"You stuck your neck out for Yancey. Sure, you can ride with me. Does your uncle know you're arriving today?" Brody closed his eyes and clenched his teeth.

"Yes, but I told him I had a ride from the airport."

"Pretty sure of me, huh?" He swallowed as his stomach dropped.

"No. I figured I'd catch a bus. You being on the same flight with me is fate." Juan laughed.

"Why'd your mom toss you out?"

"My mother kept trying to get me to change who I was." Juan shook his head. "Maybe I should have lied and told her I liked girls."

Brody relaxed as the plane levelled out. "Why didn't you? Surely you could have stayed quiet for two more years and then moved out."

"I probably should have. It would've been the easy way out, but I kept thinking about Tony and how he ran away at fifteen. He turned out all right." Juan shifted in his seat.

"I'm sure he did, but odds are he was one of the lucky ones and he'd be the first to admit it. Look how things went for Yancey. He ended up doing stuff he's probably not proud of to survive. Every adventure has two ways to go. Good or bad." Brody looked to the teenager. "Look where being honest got you. Tossed out of your house and going to live with an uncle you don't know."

Juan stared out of the window. "You're right, but lying to everyone would make me resent them more. I mean look at my *Tío* Luis."

"What about him? Who's he married to?" Brody couldn't imagine having more than one sibling.

"Luis is married to my *Tía* Angelina, *Tío* Tony's younger sister. *Mi madre's* the oldest. I saw my *Tío* Luis at a gay club in Austin. He was messing around with one of the other rent boys."

"No shit? Yet you still offered Yancey a place to stay?" Brody couldn't believe the kid would be mature enough to do that. He didn't know many adults who'd do that.

"*Tío* Luis has never had anything good to say about *Tío* Tony. He's always been nasty about gays and the clubs I visit, but he's hiding who he really is. I think his lies are making him bitter." Anger tinged Juan's voice.

He reached over and squeezed Juan's hand. "You're a great kid. Thank you for trying to give Yancey a place to recover."

"You're welcome." Juan pulled out an iPod and a set of headphones.

Brody knew Juan was done talking which was fine with him. He settled back and closed his eyes. A stray thought ran through his mind. Juan's uncle had run away from home at fifteen. It was starting to look like it wasn't just a coincidence. The next thing he knew Juan was shaking him awake.

"Hey, we're here." Juan had packed his stuff away and looked excited for the first time since Brody had met up with him that morning.

"Thank God I slept through the landing. Let's go." He stood up and they deplaned.

* * * *

Brody glanced up at the ranch house. Nothing spoke of it being owned by one of the richest men in the country. In fact, the barns and outbuildings looked to be better taken care of than the main house itself. He'd done some research online at the hotel they'd stopped at for the night. Hardin Ranch was owned by Les Hardin, a multimillionaire. He couldn't believe a man like Les would open his home to a hustler like Yancey.

He looked over to where Juan stood on the other side of the car. The teenager's wide-eyed gaze met his and he shrugged.

"May I help you?" A voice came from behind them.

Turning, Brody saw a tall man stride towards them. The man wore jeans, boots, a dark green sweatshirt, brown leather shearling jacket and a black cowboy hat.

"Yes, I'm looking for Yancey MacCafferty," Brody told him.

A bright smile gleamed on the man's face. "You must be Yancey's brother, Brody."

Brody nodded and shook the offered hand. "Yes, I am, and this is Juan, Romanos' nephew."

"Hey there, kid. I'm Jackson, Hardin's foreman. The guys are inside napping. Tony got in early this morning. Had an event in Sacramento." Jackson shoved back his hat and wiped a hand over his forehead. "Yancey was up late last night with one of my hands helping a mare foal."

A door slammed and they turned. Yancey stood on the porch. Brody's heart jumped. He wanted to be angry with his brother, but all he could feel was relief and gratitude that Yancey was okay. He covered the distance with long strides and swept his younger brother into a tight hug. Yancey held onto him and their tears mixed.

"I'm sorry," they muttered at the same time.

He hugged Yancey hard again.

"Easy there. Those ribs are healed. We don't want to break them again." A voice accented with Texas spoke from the doorway.

Brody looked up and felt his mouth drop open. He'd been right. No such thing as coincidence.

"What a God-damn small world it's turned out to be."

"You're Tony Romanos?" Brody felt his eyes widen in surprise.

"Yep. Come on inside. It's too cold outside for us to be chatting. Jackson, you coming?" Tony looked over at the foreman.

"No. I'm cleaning up and taking Tammy out for dinner." The foreman nodded at Brody and Juan. "It's nice meeting you."

Tony held the door, gesturing for the others to come in. He squeezed Juan's shoulder as his nephew went by. "We'll talk later."

Juan nodded.

Margie met them in the hall. "Yancey, Juan's in the room next to you and your brother is in the room across from Tony's. Clean up. Supper's ready and you can talk after you've eaten."

"Yes, ma'am."

Both Yancey and Tony gave the elderly lady a kiss as they went past her.

"You'll learn that even though Les owns the house, it's Margie who rules it." Tony spoke loud enough for the housekeeper to hear.

"You be respectful, cowboy, or I'll short-sheet your bed," she threatened as she went back towards the kitchen.

"She would, too." Yancey opened the door to Juan's room. "We'll share a bathroom. After dinner, I'll help grab your bags."

Brody wasn't paying much attention to the two younger men. His cock made sure his gaze remained fixed on Tony, who pointed to the fourth door on the right.

"That's your room. You'll have your own bathroom for now. The lady who stayed in the bedroom next to you moved out. Les and Randy drove her out to San Diego. They'll be back next week."

Brody stopped in front of the door. Turning, he reached out to touch Tony's face. The cowboy stepped forward and breathed deeply. Brody remembered the feel of his breath on his skin.

"I never thought I'd see you again," Brody murmured.

Tony sucked on the tip of Brody's thick thumb. He watched those blue eyes go hazy, just like he remembered in his dreams. Tony pulled away with a gentle nip.

"Neither did I, but here we are. We've got time to reunite and discuss why you told me your name was Mac." Tony pinched Brody's ass as he moved past the man. "Better wash up. Margie doesn't like serving a cold supper."

He chuckled as Tony walked down the hallway.

Twenty minutes later, they settled down at the table. Brody grinned at the amount of food Yancey and Juan put on their plates.

"Growing boys," Tony teased.

"Jackson said you helped one of his hands with a mare last night." Brody seemed determined to keep the supper conversation light.

"Yeah. It's been great. I'm thinking about going to college and vet school." Yancey flushed and looked down at the table.

"I bet you're good with animals." Juan was quick to show support.

It seemed like both Tony and Yancey waited to hear what Brody would say.

"I guess you need to decide where you want to go to school. I'll give you tuition money."

"Hell, if you wanted to stay in Wyoming, Les would probably be willing to give you a job during the summer." Tony nodded.

"Would he really do that?" Yancey sounded surprised.

"He took you in with no knowledge of who you were except what I told him." Tony chuckled. "Les is a good man. He believes in giving people help if they need it."

"I can't wait to meet Hardin." Brody passed a plate of steaks to Juan.

"Les and Randy won't be back until next week. They moved Lindsay out to California and then they were going to spend some time with Randy's older brother, Rick. He's in the Army and being deployed again." Tony didn't sound happy about Rick's leaving.

The younger men were sitting next to each other, heads tilted close together. Juan grinned at something Yancey said. Brody could see some of the tension drain from Juan's shoulders, but there was still a haunted look in his eyes.

"*Mijo*, when we're finished with the dishes, you can call *Tía* Elena and tell her you made it here okay."

"Can I call my mom, too?" Juan asked hesitantly.

"Sure, just don't be surprised if she doesn't want to talk to you."

"I know, but she's my mom and just because she doesn't treat me good doesn't mean I should act like her." Juan's chin held a stubborn tilt.

"Out of the mouths of babes. You're right, *mijo*."

Chapter Eight

They were finishing the dishes when the phone rang. Tony had sent Juan to make his calls on Tony's cell. Brody wiped the last dish dry as Tony answered the phone.

"Hey, old man, how are you doing?"

Yancey folded the towel and drained the water out of the sink. "It's Les."

"How do you know?" He was amazed by how at home his younger brother was in the house.

Yancey grabbed a soda and a beer from the fridge and led the way to the living room. Brody took the beer, sitting in an armchair. Yancey settled on the couch.

"He always gets this happy wistful tone in his voice when he talks to Randy." Yancey shrugged. "It's hard to explain. It's like he's really thrilled about being friends with the guy, but at the same time he can't help wishing it was more. To tell you the truth, though, I think he feels that way about both Les and Randy."

"Romanos wouldn't come between them, would he?" Brody didn't get that kind of impression from Tony.

"Fuck no. Their friendship means too much to him. Besides, after you meet them, you'll understand that no one will ever come between Les and Randy. It's almost sickening how perfect they are for each other." Yancey reached for a framed photograph sitting on the end table.

After putting his beer down, Brody took the picture and looked at it. Two men stood in front of a large brown horse with their arms wrapped around each other. The older, darker-haired man was taller. He had an intriguing white streak over his right temple. The shorter guy was leaner, not as handsome, but good-looking in his own right. They were smiling at the camera. Joy and love leapt from them, even though it was just paper and ink.

"Les is the one with the white streak. He used to ride jumpers in the big shows. His horse fell at a show and Les caught a hoof to the head. It was a long recovery, but he survived, got better and moved out here." Yancey pointed to the younger man. "That's Randy Hersch. He won the bareback bronc championship at the National Finals Rodeo last year. He retired and is training cutting horses here at the ranch."

"They sound like great guys." Brody set the photo down and caught his brother's eyes. "I'm sorry."

Yancey shook his head. "Nothing to be sorry about, you had to leave or you would have been killed or killed someone yourself. I know about the drugs and the gang."

"I didn't want to drag you down with me and I know if I had stayed, things would have spiraled out of control." Brody scrubbed a hand over his face. "I never meant to stay away so long. I kept meaning to come back, but there was always another job to do. I started a bodyguard business out in L.A. — it was hard, but I've got good partners and it's something I'm proud of."

Brody stood up, pacing from the sliding glass door leading out to a patio to the hallway back towards the bedrooms. "When I finally got my ass home, you were gone. Aunt Katherine told me you'd left after graduation and all I had to go on were rumours. Using my business contacts, I followed your trail to Austin. I freaked when I met Juan and learnt you had been beaten up. What the hell happened?"

He turned to see Yancey staring down at the can in his hand. "I was in the wrong place at the wrong time. Got in the middle of a gang fight. Trust me, it wasn't a gay-bashing or anything like that. I was at an all-night store, picking up some snacks and a drink. Stepped out of the store and right into the middle of a fight. I didn't have time to get out of the way. They were like a pack of rabid dogs, only interested in attacking, not caring if I was a member of either gang."

"You were turning tricks and then left for Wyoming with some stranger. What was I supposed to think?" Brody stopped at the door and stared out of it, only seeing Yancey's reflection in the window.

"Sorry. I couldn't take it anymore. Aunt Katherine is nice, but I could tell she didn't want me there, so I bailed. It was harder than I thought, surviving on the streets. I've done things I'm not proud of, but I made it this far without any lasting damage." Yancey frowned.

"You did survive and I'm proud of you for that." Brody went and sat next to his brother. "Are you okay with everything?"

Yancey knew what he was talking about. "Yeah. Les got me in to talk to a therapist. She's been helping me work through my issues."

Brody hugged the teenager. "I have a lot to thank Hardin for, I see."

"Don't forget to thank Tony. Without him, I would still be in Austin, turning tricks for rent money."

Brody shuddered at that thought.

"I couldn't believe it when Tony offered to bring me to Wyoming with him. I mean, I'm a hustler for fuck's sake." Yancey shook his head in disbelief.

"This isn't Tony's house. Why would Les let him bring a stranger here?" Brody was confused.

"Once you meet Les, you'll understand." Tony walked into the room with Juan. "Les' ranch is like a human Humane Society. The man picks up strays wherever he goes and brings them back here. He gives people a chance to get back on their feet."

"Is that how he found you?" Brody ran his gaze over Tony's compact body. He remembered the ripped abs, well-muscled arms and chest.

During the night they'd spent together, Tony had explained that upper body strength helped him gain the balance he needed to ride bulls. Brody's cock stiffened, remembering what it was like to rub against that hard stomach.

"No, he found me in a bar, playing pool with his boyfriend and sort of forcing Randy to step out of the closet for the last time." Tony chuckled.

"What would possess you to do that?" Brody reached for his beer and took a drink, leaning back next to Yancey.

Tony flung himself into a chair and Juan settled on the floor near his uncle. Brody understood the teenager's need to stay close to someone he knew wanted him around. "I didn't do it on purpose. I was going to hit on Les and wanted to know if I was stepping on any toes by doing it. Randy told me it was the moment when he had to make a decision — either admit to me that Les was indeed his boyfriend and thus out himself to me, or he could let me go and hit on Les. I know Les would have turned me down, but Randy wasn't so sure of him at the time. It ultimately was easier for him to say he was gay than to trust Les wouldn't go out with me."

"Nothing like forcing the man to sink or swim," Brody commented.

Tony laughed. "It turned out to be the best thing I could have done for both of them."

"Not many guys would think that."

"You're right, but it helped Randy. He just needed a push." He winked at Brody. "As you can tell, I'm not shy about going after what I want."

"Yeah, I remember." Brody chuckled.

Juan frowned. "Do you know each other?"

"Just to prove the world is far smaller than we thought, I happened to meet Brody in Hawaii several months ago while I was riding over there." Tony tapped Juan on the head. "We spent some time together, but I knew him as Mac."

"Mac?" Yancey stared at Brody.

"I go by Mac when I'm working," he explained to Yancey, keeping his eyes on Tony.

The bull rider nodded.

Juan yawned. Tony squeezed the teenager's shoulder.

"Yancey, why don't you help Juan get settled? It's been a long day for all of us."

Yancey stood and offered his hand to Juan, helping the dark-haired boy to his feet. Brody caught the look passing between them. There was attraction and interest in the look. He made a mental note to talk to Tony about it. The younger men wandered down the hall, laughing and talking. Tony stood as well, gesturing for Brody to follow him.

They went outside onto the porch. It was still chilly in Wyoming, so they slid on coats. Tony lit a cigarette and blew the smoke out into the night air. Brody could tell he was thinking about something.

"I thought about finding you when I was down in Austin," Tony admitted. "But the trip turned out to be shorter than I planned. Had some problems."

Brody snorted. "I can understand that. I wasn't in Dallas then. I was still in L.A.." He held out his hand and ran it over the butter-soft leather of Tony's jacket. "When I woke up that morning, I was already missing you."

Tony stubbed out his smoke and turned. Wrapping an arm around his waist, Brody pulled the shorter man to him. Their lips met in a hard kiss. Tony buried his hands in Brody's hair, keeping his mouth tight to his. Brody locked his hands behind Tony's back and brought their groins together.

"Hmm…I remember that," Tony murmured, pulling away a few inches, but grinding their hips together.

"Would you like to get reacquainted?" He winked.

"Oh, hell yes."

The eagerness in Tony's voice made Brody laugh. "Then show me to your room, cowboy."

Tony took his hand in a firm grip, leading him back through the house.

* * * *

Tony's Hawaiian one-night stand turned out to be Yancey's brother. He didn't believe in chance, but he did believe the good Lord looked after crazy cowboys and he wasn't going to miss this chance. He kept Brody close while making sure all the lights were off and the doors were locked.

The boys' doors were shut, though they heard murmurs coming from Juan's room. He nodded in their direction. Brody smiled.

"I don't think we need to worry about it at the moment," he said softly.

Tony figured Brody was right. Yancey and Juan might be attracted to each other, but they weren't going to do anything yet. His nephew was still trying to adjust to being totally out and cut off from his family. Yancey had other issues to work out. He'd keep an eye on them for now.

After pushing open his door, he pulled Brody into the room. They had hung their jackets in the laundry room off the kitchen, so all Brody wore was a dark blue sweater and jeans. Brody locked the door and reached for him. Tony went into his arms, forcing him back against the wall.

Their lips slid against each other's. He could taste the beer Brody had had after dinner. He thrust his tongue in to stroke along the roof of Brody's mouth, drawing a shiver from Brody. Tony tugged at the hem of Brody's sweater, lifting it up. They broke the kiss long enough for Tony to bare Brody's muscled chest.

He trailed kisses down Brody's neck, stopping every few inches to suck on salty flesh. He cupped Brody's firm ass and squeezed. Brody dropped his head back, offering the tanned expanse of his torso to Tony's mouth.

Stepping back, Tony hooked a finger in Brody's waistband and urged him to move. "We need to get naked and take this to the bed."

Passion-glazed blue eyes gleamed at him. "I like those words—naked and bed."

"Good. There have been a few nights I imagined you in that bed with me."

"What were we doing?" Brody's fingers brushed his as Brody started to unbutton his jeans.

"Exactly what we'll be doing in a few minutes." He stripped, not wasting any more time.

Brody did the same and Tony leered at the man's extraordinary body. The muscles were defined and strong. He laid a hand on Brody's ripped abs and smiled. Brody's entire body spoke of health and exercise. It was clear the man took care of himself and Tony was happy to be reaping the rewards of all that diligent work.

He leant forward, fastening his lips around one of the flat copper nipples, and Brody gasped. After flicking the bit of flesh with his tongue, he pinched it tight between his teeth and tugged. Brody's back arched as he threaded his hands through Tony's hair to hold his mouth tight to Brody's chest. Tony teased and sucked until the nipple was red. He moved to the other nipple, making sure it didn't feel left out.

"God," Brody moaned.

Tony slid his hands down and around to grip Brody's tight ass. He traced a line through the crease, caressing the opening hidden there. The puckered ring fluttered as he rubbed over it. Pulling his finger away, he held it up to Brody's mouth. Brody sucked it in, bathing it with his spit. Tony took it out with a pop and reached behind Brody again.

He pressed his finger in as deep as he could with one single thrust. Brody groaned, pushing their hips together. The pre-cum leaking from their cocks painted their stomachs. Tony moved them to the bed, stroking his finger in and out before withdrawing it completely.

"On the bed," he ordered.

Brody climbed up on the mattress, propping his body on his hands and knees. Tony dug around his nightstand, searching for the lube he'd thrown in there earlier. He closed his fingers closed around the plastic tube along with a foil package. Good thing he'd just emptied everything from his shaving kit into the drawer. He knelt behind Brody, leaning forward to lick a line along the man's spine.

"Fuck. Just do it already." Brody arched, his voice strained.

Tony chuckled. Nothing made him hotter than having his lover beg for him. After squeezing the slick lube onto his fingers, he circled Brody's hole with it. He spread Brody's ass cheeks with one hand while pressing the tip of one finger into his tight passage.

"I couldn't stop thinking about you," Brody admitted.

Burying his finger deep enough to nail Brody's gland, Tony smiled at the full-body shiver racking the man. He leant forward and nibbled at the soft skin at the top of Brody's crease, twisting his finger to brush that same special spot again.

"Come on, Tony. Don't tease me," Brody begged.

He inserted two more fingers, scissoring them to stretch and relax the ring of muscle. Brody's head dropped forward and his body rocked back. Tony braced himself against Brody's hip, reached around with his other hand and fisted Brody's erection. He swiped his palm through the pre-cum leaking from the slit in Brody's bulbous cock head, using the liquid to help ease the friction as he stroked the shaft in his hand.

He pressed his lips against Brody's ear. "You've got a big thick cock. I loved how it stretched me and filled my ass when you fucked me." He shoved three fingers in and rubbed the gland. "I dreamed of sinking my cock into your tight ass. Can you remember how it felt?"

Brody groaned, humping his hand. "Romanos. Damn it, just fuck me now."

Tony pulled away and grabbed the condom. He tore the foil package open before tugging the rubber out. He rolled it over his cock then knelt behind Brody. He popped open the tube and squirted some more lube on his fingers. He rubbed it between them, warming it, then slipped his fingers into Brody's tight passage, but he didn't do much except make sure Brody was still stretched. Pulling out, he poured more liquid in his palm and coated his own cock with it.

"Ready?" He caressed the firm ass cheek before him.

"Yes," Brody hissed through clenched teeth.

Chuckling, he lined his cock up with Brody's hole and pushed in with a steady stroke. He didn't ease off or stop until he was buried balls deep. They both grunted as Brody clenched his muscles around Tony's dick. He slid out until only an inch of his cock remained inside.

"No," Brody protested.

He slammed back in, skin slapping skin. His cock nailed Brody's gland, making his lover moan. Soon, they were rocking in the carnal dance. Tony loved fucking almost as much as he loved riding bulls.

The base of his spine tingled and his balls drew tight to his body. Reaching around, he started stroking again, hard and fast. His actions blended until Brody begged him to let him come. He leant forward, squeezed the cock in his hand and bit Brody's shoulder.

Wet heat covered his hand and Brody's ass clamped down on his cock, drawing his own climax from him. With a grunt, he froze and filled the condom. He collapsed on top of Brody, whose arms gave out, and they flopped to the bed.

Tony rolled off the bed before heading towards the bathroom. He tied off then threw away the condom. After grabbing a washcloth, he cleaned up and went back to wipe Brody down as well. He tossed the cloth back into the sink then he climbed back in bed, snuggling tight to Brody.

"I should go back to my room," Brody mumbled.

"Why?" He wrapped an arm around Brody's waist.

"The boys."

"Trust me, those boys know more about sex than you and I did at their age. They aren't going to be shocked to see you leave my room tomorrow morning." He nuzzled Brody's neck, tasting the salt off his skin.

A soft chuckle shook Brody's body. "You're right."

"Always am."

His eyes drifted shut and he relaxed, listening to Brody's breathing even out. The sex was as hot as he remembered. He stroked his hand over Brody's skin. It was crazy how much he wanted this man, but he wasn't completely sold on his returning for Yancey. Brody spoke all the right words about wanting the younger man to be happy, but they would see how long it lasted. For now, he would give the benefit of the doubt.

Chapter Nine

The door slammed open, causing both Brody and Tony to sit up in surprise.

"What the hell?" Tony glared at the dark-haired man standing in the doorway.

"Oops. Sorry. Didn't know you had a friend staying over." The man grinned and winked at Brody. "Hi, I'm Randy Hersch."

Brody shook the rough hand held out to him, still trying to shake the sleep from his mind. "I'm Brody MacCafferty."

"Yancey's brother?" Randy frowned and perched on the edge of the mattress.

"Yes." He shot a glance over at Tony.

Tony had lain back down on his side with the pillow bunched under his head. He didn't seem too surprised Randy seemed to have settled in for a chat.

"When did you get in?" Randy enquired.

"Yesterday. I brought Tony's nephew, Juan, with me." He leant back against the headboard and pulled the sheet up, crossing his arms over his chest.

"Juan's here as well?" Randy glared at Tony. "You didn't say anything about him coming."

"I didn't know, though I told Les it was a possibility." Tony reached out and trailed fingers over Brody's arm.

"Told me what?" A honeyed voice drifted into the room.

Brody looked up to see a tall, older man move through the doorway. He had a white streak over his right temple. This had to be Les Hardin. Les stood behind Randy, resting a hand on his shoulder. Les grinned at him.

"He told you Juan might be coming to stay?" Randy's voice held a question.

"Oh, right. He did. I forgot to tell you in all the rush to get to the airport and everything." Les brushed a kiss over Randy's cheek.

"Hmm...I'll let it pass for now." Randy looked back at Brody. "So how long are you staying?"

"Umm..." He wasn't sure what to say.

Les laughed. "Randy, how about we go and leave these two alone to wake up without you staring at them? You can be nosy all you want at breakfast." Hardin tugged Randy to his feet, winking at Brody and Tony. "We'll see you in a few minutes."

"Thanks, Les. Can you check and see if the boys are up?" Tony stretched.

"Yancey is. He's out helping Jackson and the hands with the horses." Les dragged Randy out of the room before shutting the door behind him.

"That was Randy and Les, if you hadn't figured it out." Tony crawled out of bed to pad towards the bathroom.

Brody eyed Tony's firm bubble butt, his cock aching to be buried in it. He threw the sheet off then strolled over to the bull rider. Snaking his arm around Tony's lean waist, he tugged the man back tight to him, his cock nestling in Tony's crease.

Pressing his lips to Tony's ear, he said, "Where do you think you're going?"

"I'm going to take a shower." Tony rubbed against him. "You're welcome to join me. It'll save on water."

"Environmentally conscious, that's me." He slid one hand down to cup Tony's balls, fondling them with rough fingers.

"Let's go before someone else decides to burst in on us." Tony gripped his hand and led him to the shower.

He leaned against the sink, watching Tony place a condom and lube on the shelf in the shower stall. His lover leered at him over his shoulder and Brody crowded Tony under the water. The hot spray poured over their bodies, slicking their skins. He grabbed the soap and lathered his hands, running them over the muscles he'd fantasised about for months.

Tony stretched and turned, allowing Brody to touch him wherever he wanted. Gripping Tony's hips, he pinned the man to the tiled wall and knelt down. Tony threaded his fingers into Brody's hair, massaging and petting. Glancing up, Brody grinned then swallowed Tony's cock down to the base.

"Fuck." The back of Tony's head slammed against the wall.

Wrapping one hand around Tony's cock, Brody pumped and stroked while he sucked. He trailed the fingers of his other hand down Tony's crease, teasing the puckered opening. He applied a little pressure and eased his finger in up to the first knuckle.

"M-m-m..." Tony arched up, rocking between Brody's mouth and finger.

One finger became two, then three. He sucked and swallowed, jacking his lover off. He flexed his fingers, stretching the hole so his cock would slide into Tony without problem.

"Soon," Tony warned.

Brody knew that. The pre-cum leaking out of Tony's cock coated his tongue. He removed his mouth from Tony's shaft before bending lower then sucked on the inside of Tony's thigh while pumping. He slipped his fingers in and out, doing his best to nail Tony's gland with every thrust.

"Brody," Tony grunted and warmth flowed over Brody's hand.

He waited until Tony's cock softened before he stood up. Offering his hand to Tony, he moaned as the other man licked the cum off his fingers.

"Turn around," he ordered, reaching for the condom Tony had left on the shelf.

Tony winked at him and turned, bracing his hands on the tiles. Those lean hips tilted. After rolling the rubber on, Brody caressed Tony's firm ass and used one hand to spread the cheeks. He found the lube, squirted some onto Tony's hole and massaged it in.

"Come on, Brody. I want you in me." Tony shoved back and clenched his ass around Brody's fingers.

"All right, cowboy. Just a second." He grabbed the slick stuff again and coated his cock.

Placing his cock at Tony's opening, he pushed in while Tony rocked back. He paused at the moment when he was buried to the balls in Tony. The tanned expanse of Tony's back moved beneath him. He leant forward and licked the man's spine, enjoying the rough moan that issued from his lover.

"God, Brody."

He knew what Tony wanted. He pulled out until only an inch of his cock rested inside Tony's passage. Gripping the man's hips, he slammed back in.

"Fuck." Tony's head dropped forward.

"That's what we're doing." Brody chuckled.

"Funny. Just do me." Tony glared back at him.

He slapped Tony's ass then proceeded to ream him. From the way Tony jerked, Brody assumed he nailed the man's gland with each slide in. He freed one of his hands from Tony's hip and wrapped it around the thick cock standing proud at Tony's groin. Brody knew it wouldn't take long to drive Tony over the edge again.

"Ah," Tony groaned. Heat spilled over Brody's fingers.

"Shit," Brody shouted, as Tony's inner passage clamped down on him and milked his own climax from him. He held Tony still while he filled the condom.

Brody braced one of his hands next to Tony's on the wall, trying not to collapse into a puddle on the shower's floor. When he managed to calm his breathing, he pulled out, then tied off the condom before cleaning them both up. He turned the water off and helped Tony out of the shower.

Tony blinked at him. "How long are you going to stay?"

"For a few days. I'll need to get back to L.A., I have a business to run." Brody grabbed a towel and started to dry off.

"What about Yancey? You can't just leave him again." Tony frowned.

"I wasn't planning on abandoning him. He and I'll stay in touch. If he wanted to, I'd welcome him to come and live with me." Brody smiled. "He seems happy here, Tony, and I don't want anything more than that for him."

Tony studied him. "I think you actually mean that."

"I do."

His lover nodded and smiled. "I think I want to go back and sleep a little longer."

"You could if you wanted to, I guess." He brushed a kiss over Tony's mouth. "I'm going to get breakfast. All this sex is making me hungry."

The bull rider sighed. "You're right, and we don't want Randy coming back in. Sorry about that."

"He's your friend. Have you had many guys spend the night?" Brody went into the bedroom and grimaced. "I have to go to my room and get dressed."

"You could just bring your bag in here. No one's going to have a problem with us sharing a bed." Tony tugged a pair of sweats and a T-shirt on. "You're the first guy I've ever brought here."

Brody tucked the towel around his waist and headed across the hall to the guest room. After dressing, he sat on the edge of the mattress. Brody stared at his hands and wondered what the hell he was doing.

He'd come to Wyoming to re-connect with his brother, not fall into bed with a cowboy. He liked Tony, enjoyed the sex and found the man attractive in so many ways, but Tony wasn't the most important part of the equation. Yancey was.

A noise made him look up. Yancey leaned against the doorframe and smiled at him.

"Sleep well?"

Heat filled his cheeks and he ducked his head. Hell, why was he embarrassed? He was an adult and could sleep wherever he wanted. "Yes, I did."

Yancey chuckled and joined him on the bed. "Why are you blushing?"

Brody shrugged. "I don't know. Stupid, isn't it? Considering what you've been doing in Austin."

"Yeah, but I don't want to think about my brother like that."

"You know, Tony was the first one-night stand I'd had in a while. Been too busy working and building up my company. I didn't have time to meet anyone and I'd never buy sex." He grinned at his younger brother.

"Company?" Yancey glanced at him. "Oh right, your bodyguard business."

"Personal security. We started out as bodyguards, but now we're branching out to security systems and things like that." He sat back on the bed, leaning against the headboard.

"We?"

"Morgan Kozlov and Vance Gladstone. We were bouncers at a nightclub when I first hit Los Angeles. Hung around together all the time and decided that being bodyguards might be more profitable for all of us. Word got around. We picked up a few clients. It's been going well the last year or so. We've trained a few other guys and we're getting more business." Brody studied his brother. "I know last night you said you wanted to go to college and maybe become a vet."

"I enjoy working with the horses." Yancey walked to the window and stared outside. "First time in a year or so that I know what I want to do."

"I won't stop you if that's really what you want to do, but would you like to come out to L.A. and spend some time with me there? I need to get back in a couple of days."

His brother turned to look at him. "Really? What about you and Tony?"

He clenched his hands in his lap. "I'm not going to lie and say the sex isn't great. I wouldn't mind seeing him again, but I can't stay here and he's not really going to want to move out to L.A., just on the off chance he and I might hit it off."

"I understand. Do you think we can hang around here for a few days and then I could come and check out your town?"

He and Yancey exchanged a smile. "Sure. I'd like to get to know Les and Randy as well. They sound like great guys."

"Cool." Yancey held out a hand to help Brody to his feet. His brother leaned in and whispered, "I'd like to spend some time with Juan."

"Those Romanos genes are pretty remarkable, aren't they?"

He followed Yancey out and down the hall. Instead of the dining room where they'd eaten the night before, they went into the kitchen where a long table was set up in an alcove. Juan, Jackson and Tony were already there. Randy was helping Margie carrying platters of food. Les came in behind them, talking to a thin younger man.

"Thought you fell asleep," Tony joked as Brody sat down next to him.

"It passed through my mind." He winked at his lover.

"I didn't get a chance to introduce myself. I'm Les Hardin and this is my accountant, Peter Skinner." He gestured to the man who'd come in with him. "You've met my partner, Randy, and my housekeeper, Margie."

Brody offered his hand to Les. "I want to thank both of you for letting Yancey come and stay with you."

Les' grip was firm. "You're welcome. Our home is open to anyone who needs a place to stay."

"They pick up a lot of strays." Tony shot Randy a wink.

"I hope you're not complaining, since you're one of them." Randy set a plate of eggs and bacon down in front of Brody. "Sorry about busting in on you like that." A blush tinged Randy's cheeks.

"It's all right." He shifted, still a little uncomfortable about it. "The guys I share a place with out in L.A. have been known to do the same thing."

"You're living in L.A., huh? We just got back from San Diego. Moved a friend out there and hung out with Randy's older brother." Les waited until Margie sat down before he started eating.

"It's nice. We own a personal security business. There isn't a better place in the world for bodyguards than L.A.." He noticed how Yancey and Juan were whispering, heads together. "What do you guys raise?"

"A little bit of everything." Les snorted. "Cutting and bucking horses. Beef cattle and bucking bulls. Randy helps with the rough stock breeding and he trains the cutting horses. I've started doing private clinics for show riders. Jumpers mostly."

"Plus he has his hands in a bunch of other cookie jars. Ask Peter there. I think being Les' accountant must be driving him to the edge." Randy nodded towards the quiet blond man.

"I like the challenge," Peter said softly.

"He's teasing." Les reached over and tapped the accountant's hand. Turning back to Brody, Les asked, "So how long are you staying?"

"A couple days and then I have to head back. Yancey said he'd go out there with me."

Juan looked upset and Yancey touched the younger man's arm. Brody shot a glance at Tony, who smiled at him.

"I'm still thinking about going to college at the University of Wyoming. I haven't seen Brody for five years. Figured I could spend some time with him." Yancey seemed to be reassuring Juan.

"If you want work here during breaks when you're not visiting Brody, you're welcome. You can work with the animals. Learn some things from the hands. If your brother's fine with it, I don't have a problem." Les shrugged.

Brody chuckled. "Yancey's been taking care of himself for a while now. I don't think I have any right to start telling him what to do now."

He jumped when Tony squeezed his thigh. Talk welled up around him as Randy and Les caught up with ranch business.

After breakfast, Les, Randy and Jackson grabbed their coats and headed back outside. Peter muttered a distracted goodbye, disappearing down a hall.

Yancey looked at Juan. "Want to help Margie with the dishes and then I'll show you around the ranch?"

Juan nodded. The boys wandered off, still whispering together. Brody sipped his coffee and met Tony's gaze. He gestured towards the younger men.

"Interesting dynamic there."

Tony grinned. "It'll be fun to watch how it plays out. Though I don't think either one of them is ready to commit to one person. Yancey has a few more issues to work out."

"I'm looking forward to having him come out to L.A. with me, but I don't want him living there. It's too easy to get swept up in the scene." Brody shook his head. "I think you and the other guys will give him a better perspective on things. Plus I'd like him to hang out with Juan."

"Juan's a good kid. Even if his mom can't see that." Tony pushed away from the table. "You want to take a walk with me? I'm going to check out the rough stock. Les said Burt and Dusty brought a couple new bulls back from an auction."

"Sure, but you'll have to give me a crash course on bull riding and rodeo." Brody grinned.

"No problem."

He pulled on his jacket and boots, waiting for Tony to change into jeans and a sweatshirt. Hearing laughter, he stuck his head in the kitchen and saw the boys in the middle of a water fight. He ducked back out, grabbing Tony as the man started to go past him.

"I wouldn't go in there if I were you. Margie's going to have a fit when she sees what they've done." Brody explained what the boys had been up to.

Tony dragged him out of the house. "She'll make them clean up the entire room." Tony wrapped his arm around Brody's waist.

Brody glanced around at the ranch hands wandering through the yard. None of them glanced at them or said a word about seeing two guys walking arm-in-arm.

"Don't worry. None of the guys who work here are going to say anything about us. Les won't allow prejudice here. He says it's bad enough he has to pretend and not touch Randy when they're in public. He refuses to do that at home. Makes things easier, in a way." Tony snuggled closer to him.

He put his arm around Tony's shoulder as they made their way to the first barn. He'd take advantage of any opportunity to hold Tony's compact body. Les, Randy and Jackson stood by one of the stalls, talking softly. He dropped back while Tony joined the trio.

Both Randy and Les welcomed the bull rider in. Les put his hand on Tony's shoulder. Randy included Tony in his personal space. Studying the dynamics between the men, Brody could tell that even though Les and Randy were the couple and very much in love, a deep friendship existed between them and Tony.

Not wanting to eavesdrop on the conversation, he turned to look at the horse in the stall he was standing in front of. Brody didn't know anything about horses, but this one was an imposing specimen. Its coat was a burnished copper and he had a long black mane and tail. Large liquid black eyes stared at him. He got the feeling the horse was tense, like it was bracing for him to make a move. When he didn't do anything, the horse snorted and moved towards him.

"He's looking for this." Les reached around him, holding out a piece of carrot.

"What breed is he?" He watched the horse take the carrot from Les' palm and munch happily.

"He's a Thoroughbred. He's here for training right now. I can't compete anymore, but I still know how to ride." Les shrugged. "I used to be the best in the country and there are people willing to listen to me."

"I thought Thoroughbreds were race horses." He reached out a hand and then froze. "Is it all right if I pet him?"

"Sure. Boo is a perfect example of a Thoroughbred and he expects us all to worship him." Les stroked the inquisitive Boo's nose.

Brody caressed the soft space between Boo's eyes and scratched the horse's neck under the mane. "Are you going to train him?"

"No. His rider's coming in a couple days. Edward was the first person to come and ask me to help him with his horses. His main ride, Gypsy's Salt Mine, is injured and has to be rested for a month or so. Edward wants to work with Boo. I think he has plenty of talent." Les nudged Brody with his shoulder. "Talent doesn't mean anything. He has to have the will to jump and take those fences with speed and power. I haven't taken him over any jumps."

Randy joined them. "I won't let him."

Brody glanced over at the younger man. "Why not?"

"I have to be careful. If I hit my head just right, I could do serious damage." Les tapped the side of his head where a white streak of hair covered a concave spot.

"We don't want that to happen." Tony slid next to Brody, encircling Brody's waist with his arm.

"So where are your Quarter Horses?" Brody asked Randy.

Randy gestured down the aisle towards the stalls at the other end of the barn. "The ones in training are at the end of this barn. The mares and the yearlings are in the next barn over. Then there's the smaller barn with Les' horse, Sam, and a few others we don't really use, but just enjoy having around."

"Do you have a star horse?" He rested his chin on Tony's shoulder.

"All of the horses on this ranch are stars in Les' eyes," Tony teased, tugging him ahead. "You should see some of these horses. None of them except the ones brought in by his clients are going to win any conformation classes. Even more of Les' strays."

"I haven't heard you complain." Les pinched Tony's ass.

Brody laughed as Tony squeaked. They stopped in front of another stall. Les nodded at the grey standing in the middle of the stall.

"This is our newest star, Hardin Ranch's Folsom."

Brody grimaced at the scars covering the grey's muscular body. "He's had a rough life, hasn't he?"

"Yeah, but he just needed someone to treat him good." The grey stuck his nose over the door and nuzzled Randy's chest.

"Here you go, baby." Les handed Randy another carrot. "Story of our lives. We all need someone to treat us good."

He had the feeling Les spoke from experience. His nod encouraged Randy to go into detail about Folsom's training schedule. After five minutes, he knew his eyes had glazed over because he didn't understand a word of what Randy was saying.

"Give it up, cowboy. Brody doesn't know a thing about horses, or cutting classes either." Tony laughed. "He might be from Texas, but he's a city boy."

"I haven't heard you complain about my lack of ranch knowledge," Brody challenged Tony.

"Oh, it's not your knowledge of horses I'm after. It's your expert knowledge of sucking cock I want." Tony sprinted out of the barn.

Randy and Les were doubled over, laughing hysterically while Brody stared at them wide-eyed. He couldn't believe the bull rider had said that. He took off after Tony and tackled him right before the man made it to the porch and safety.

They fell headfirst into the snowdrift. Brody landed on his back, cushioning Tony from the worst of the snow. After getting a face full of cold, wet flakes, he rolled so he was lying on top of Tony and grinning.

Chapter Ten

Tony sucked in a sharp breath as the cold seeped in through his jeans and jacket. He stared up into Brody's blue eyes and saw the twinkle in them. He bucked his hips, arching and tossing the man off him, just in time to catch a snowball flush in the face.

"Shit. You weren't supposed to do that, Tony." Randy's laughter-filled voice made him look over at his friend. Randy stood, leaning against Les, mirth making it hard for the man to stand up.

Brody chuckled. "If you were in L.A., you wouldn't be having this problem."

A snowball smacked Brody chest high and dead centre. Both Tony and Brody turned to see Les bent over, making another one. Tony winked at Brody and they both reached for snow.

Soon all four men were covered head to toe in snow. Yells and shouts filled the air. At some point, Juan and Yancey had joined in. Juan had never played in the snow, so everyone helped him experience it. With their help, a lopsided snowman was built, and Tony's cowboy hat rested on top of it. They stole a carrot out of the refrigerator for the nose.

Tony nudged Brody as Yancey wrapped his arm around Juan to share body heat.

"Go back inside and change your clothes, boys." Les pushed Yancey back towards the house. "Don't need you to catch colds. Especially if Juan is going to have to enrol in school on Monday."

"Fuck. I forgot about that," Tony mumbled as they all headed inside.

"Don't worry. Your aunt made sure Juan had all his papers and stuff in order. Just in case something happens," Brody told him. "Hey, Juan, don't forget to give Tony that packet of papers you brought."

"Gotcha." Juan waved, acknowledging Brody's words as he disappeared into his bedroom.

All the guys separated, changing their clothes and trying to warm up. Tony buttoned his jeans and sat down on his bed, staring down at his feet. The thought of what he was about to take on struck him.

He looked up as Brody peeked into the room.

"You coming?"

"Yeah, in a minute." He went back to studying his feet.

Brody frowned and joined him on the bed. The extra weight caused a dip in the mattress and Tony tilted to rest against Brody's bigger body.

"What's wrong?" Brody took his hand then rested their entwined fingers on his own thigh.

"It just hit me. I'm going to be Juan's parent." He met Brody's eyes. "What the hell was I thinking?"

Brody cupped his cheek with his free hand. "You were thinking about the support you never got and how you wouldn't allow Juan to go without family. You remembered how you felt."

"I've never dealt with teenagers. What am I supposed to do? How do I teach him to be an adult when I'm not even sure I am?" He gripped Brody's hand, suddenly feeling overwhelmed.

"You'll be fine. Randy and Les will be here to help you out. I know Yancey isn't going to be walking away from Juan, though that might change a little when he goes to college." Brody dropped a kiss on Tony's lips. "I'm only a phone call away as well."

"What good are you going to be to me? You've never raised a kid." He frowned. "Or have you?"

Brody shook his head. "I messed around with a girl or two when I was in high school, but even then I knew about condoms."

"Ewww, you kissed a girl?" He wrinkled his nose in mock disgust.

"It wasn't bad. Just wasn't what got me hot and bothered. Now, the guys on the football team? That was a whole other story." His lover leered at him then a serious expression crossed Brody's face. "What I meant is you can call me when Juan makes you angry. Trust me, he will. Teenage boys can't help that. You call me and yell at me. That way, you can go talk to him like a rational person instead of a raving lunatic."

"You don't think I'm going to screw this up and ruin his life even more, do you?" Tony didn't know why he was looking for reassurance, but he needed someone to tell him he'd do a good job.

"How can you screw up his life?" Brody stood, pulled Tony to his feet and hugged him. "He gets to see that, for the most part, a gay man can live a normal life without being ashamed of who he is. At least here on Les' ranch, he'll be able to be himself. You'll make him strong enough to live on his terms, not his mother's, or anyone else's either."

"Thanks. I needed that." He buried his face in the spot at the base of Brody's neck and breathed in Brody's warm, spicy scent.

"Come on. You still have to show me the rough stock." Brody stepped away from him.

He let the blond drag him from his bedroom. They put on dry coats then went back outside to check out the other animals. Tony wanted to try a couple of the bulls. It had been a week since he'd ridden and he was going to miss the next two events getting Juan settled in. Dusty and Burt met him in the indoor arena where the bucking chutes were.

The two retired bull riders were in charge of Les' bucking bull programme and were friends of Randy's from the rodeo circuit.

"Dusty. Burt. This is Brody MacCafferty, Yancey's older brother." Tony walked over to check out the three bulls standing in the chutes. "New ones?"

"Got delivered while you were away." The smaller of the two men shook Brody's hand. "Dusty Spiess. Knew Tony and Randy out on the circuit while we were competing. This is my partner, Burt Tackett."

"Does Les advertise in gay magazines to get you all to come out here? Or are all the rumours true about cowboys?" Brody joked.

Burt laughed. "Does seem to be a lot of us concentrated here, but trust me, the majority of the hands and cowboys you'll meet around here are straight. The guys on the ranch won't give you any trouble. The guys you meet in town might be a different story."

"I appreciate the warning. Living in L.A. gives a person a rather jaded sense of the world. I understand not every place is as open-minded, so I won't kiss Tony in public." Brody nodded.

"Well, shit. You give him any more warnings, Burt, I won't be getting any sex from him." Tony winked at the men.

Brody shook his head while the two older cowboys chuckled.

"You are shameless, Romanos." Dusty cuffed his head as the man walked past. "Let's get your rig on Megabeef there."

"Megabeef? He's a bit on the short side." He looked at the bull with scepticism.

The bull was shorter than most he'd ridden and looked skinnier.

"Yep. He's only a four year old and doesn't ship well. He'll fill out, put some inches on and he'll be a good one." Burt nudged Brody. "Isn't it a little like the kettle calling the pot black?"

Tony shot Burt a scowl while he climbed up on the gate and straddled the top, one foot resting on a bar at each side of the bull. Brody leaned against the far fence, watching as Tony tightened the rope around the bull's stomach.

"What's he doing?" Brody nodded towards Tony.

"He's wrapping his bull rope. To be able to stay on the bull for eight seconds, a cowboy needs to have something to hold on to."

"Isn't that cheating? Wouldn't having something to hang on to make it easier to stay on?" Brody shook his head, puzzled.

"Wait until you see them buck. The cowboys need all the help they can get to stick to these animals." Burt gestured to the rope. "If you notice, a section of the rope has a kind of a handle on it. Tony'll fit his hand in the handle and then wrap a section of the bull rope around his hand. He tucks it under his fingers, making sure it's as tight as possible."

Megabeef kicked the chute when Tony lowered himself down on the bull's back. Brody jumped. The bull bellowed and tossed its head, flinging snot all over the gate. Nervousness shot through Brody. Having never seen any sort of rodeo, he was worried about Tony.

No matter how much the others spoke about Megabeef being small for a bull, the animal still looked huge to Brody. What kind of person thought it was fun to get on the back of a one-ton animal and try to ride it for eight seconds?

"What's the bell for?" He pointed to the cowbell hanging from the rope under the bull's stomach.

"It adds weight to the rope. When the cowboy pulls the tail of the rope free, it allows the rigging to fall off. That way the rider can get off, but also doesn't have to chase the bull into the bull pen to get his gear back."

Brody nodded. "Why do this? Why ride bulls?"

Burt shrugged. "Why do people jump out of airplanes or drive fast cars? It's a matter of adrenaline and fear. Also, when you make it to eight seconds without taking a header off the bull, you know you've accomplished something most people never have."

"I still think it's the craziest thing I've ever seen."

The ex-bull rider chuckled. "You're right there. It is crazy, but it's becoming one of the most popular sports in the country."

The chute banged open and Megabeef exploded from the gate. His first leap out landed them ten feet from the chute. The bull ducked to the left and spun. Tony sat tight, rocking his hips with the movement of the bull's kicks. Bellowing, the brindle bull stopped, shot to the right with a huge jump and gave a belly roll to try to dislodge the man on his back.

"Fuck, that brindle is rank." Burt whistled.

Tony slid to the left. His free arm flailed as the cowboy tried to find his balance again.

"Megabeef has him back off his rope and off balance. That's never a good combination." Burt winked at Brody.

Another quick stop, but this time the bull shot sideways to the right, leaving Tony face first in the dirt. Brody started forward to help Tony, but Burt's arm shot across Brody's chest, stopping him.

"Let James get the bull out of the arena." Burt nodded over to where a young man herded the brindle animal towards the large gate.

Tony scrambled to his feet and ran over to Brody. He wore a huge grin, flung his arms around Brody's waist and gave him a big hug.

"Wasn't that awesome?" Tony let go and spun around to Burt. "He'll be great when he gains weight and gets a little bigger."

Burt agreed. "I thought so. Take a minute to catch your breath while we run the next one in."

Brody checked out Tony's ass, framed by his black leather chaps. Reaching out, he palmed one of those firm cheeks and squeezed. Tony gasped and pushed back.

Brody leant down to whisper in Tony's ear. "I think I'll be fantasising about you riding me while wearing these."

Tony pressed tight to him, rubbing his bubble butt against Brody's groin. They both moaned.

"Stop it, you two. There's innocent kids around and you can't be riding with a hard-on," Dusty shouted from the chutes.

Brody nipped Tony's earlobe before letting the bull rider go and turning around to smile at the older men. "I don't think you've seen young or innocent in a long time, Dusty."

The red-haired cowboy flipped him the finger and Brody laughed, slapping Tony's ass.

"Get up there and show me how it's done."

Tony shot a smirk over his shoulder at Brody and sauntered up to the bucking chute, swinging his hips like a slut. Brody whistled low. The other men were doubled over, cackling.

Brody climbed to the platform built at one end of the indoor arena. He settled in one of the chairs and watched. Randy arrived to help get Tony ready to ride. Brody studied the two men and wondered about the dynamics between them. They were comfortable with each other, like long-time friends or old lovers would be. He felt an unwelcome surge of jealousy. It was a stupid emotion, especially since he'd only slept with Tony twice and didn't really know the man at all.

"They never were."

He glanced around to see Les standing at the back of the platform, resting a hip against the railing. Brody wanted to pretend he didn't know what Les was talking about, but neither of them were stupid.

"I'm that obvious, huh?"

The corner of Les' thin mouth lifted slightly. "Just a little. No one else would notice if they weren't looking for it."

Les made his way around the chairs to sit next to him. Les studied their lovers for a moment before turning to look at Brody. He was startled by the intense stare he received from Les. He wanted to shift or straighten his shirt. He wanted to do anything to stop the man from peering into his soul.

"We don't get to meet Tony's lovers." Les looked away when Randy's laughter drifted from the other side of the arena.

"You wouldn't have met me if Yancey hadn't become friends with Juan." Brody snorted. "Strange coincidence."

Les shrugged. "I don't believe in coincidence. Everything happens for the right reason at the right time. Tony and Randy are good friends, probably best friends in many ways."

"Really?"

After climbing up, Tony settled down on the back of a large red bull. Randy leaned over the side of the chute, his hands under the vest Tony was wearing.

"They both lived in a world where they couldn't be themselves. For the most part, Randy is out of the rodeo circuit, but he still is careful about who he tells or shows. Tony lives in that world and though he's managed to find ways around the restrictions put on him, he's very much in the closet." Les settled back and rested his right ankle on his left knee. "They understand each other better than I could ever begin to."

"You never hid who you were." Brody could see that.

There was an air of confidence in the way Les walked and moved that spoke of Les' surety of his place in the world. Brody figured that even after his accident and getting dumped by his lover, Les had never really doubted who or what he was.

"Didn't have to. As long as I rode well, people didn't care who I loved. It didn't make me less of a man in their eyes." Les nodded towards the others. "They're good men or I wouldn't have them working for me.

Yet there are ones who believe if you fuck men or get fucked by them, you're less male than a straight guy."

"I've never understood that philosophy."

"Doesn't have to make sense." Les shook his head. "It just takes someone believing it."

"True." He held his breath as the red bull burst from the chute and spun to the right.

He found his body moving with each rocking motion that Tony made. His lungs burned and his hands were clenched on his thighs. A buzzer rang and Tony tugged on the tail of his rope, unhooking his hand from the hemp. Dusty and Burt flagged the bull, getting it to spin left so Tony could bail out to the right without getting stomped on. Brody's breath hissed from his chest when Tony sprang from the dirt and waved at him.

"Don't hurt him."

Surprised, he turned to Les, who wasn't looking at him. Les waved to Tony, a laugh bursting from Les as Randy raced over and tackled Tony.

"I would think you'd be more worried about his chosen profession than me hurting him." Brody stood.

"I always worry when he rides, but his body will heal. If you break his heart, I'm not sure if he would be as giving as he is now."

"You give me more power than I have. I'm a one-night stand he got to see again. Besides, if he is hurt, he has you and Randy to comfort him." He started to leave the platform, but he stopped and turned back to Les. "Tony's a lucky man to have people who care so much for him."

Les bowed his head, acknowledging the compliment.

Brody caught Tony as he threw himself at him. Tony's bright smile burned through Brody's chest and touched his heart. He realised he wanted to see Tony as happy and relaxed as he was now forever.

"Did you see me ride that bastard?" Tony wrapped his arms around Brody's neck and kissed him.

Brody held Tony's compact body tight to his and kissed him back. Their mouths fused, the kiss going deeper and hotter. Tongues tangled. Teeth nibbled. A moan rose from one of their throats—neither knew which one it came from. Brody slid his hands down to cup Tony's ass and rocking their hips together.

"Hey, you two. Don't make me get some snow to cool you off."

A voice broke through the heat of desire, pulling them back to reality. Brody let go and stepped away, his cheeks hot and chest heaving slightly. He'd met a few guys who could turn him on in an instant, but none had made him forget where he was. He turned to see Randy grinning at them.

Tony shot his friend the finger, but didn't move away from Brody. "There have been plenty of times I thought I'd have to hose you and Les down, cowboy. Don't make me come over there and kick your ass."

"Like you could," Randy dared him.

Brody shook his head as Tony took off after Randy, chasing him around the arena.

"And then there are times when I think they're brothers separated at birth."

Les' amused comment caused Brody to laugh. It wasn't time to worry about their relationship. He still had time before he had to go back to L.A.. His cell phone rang, interrupting his enjoyment of watching Tony and Randy wrestling in the dirt.

"MacCafferty," he barked into the phone.

"Hey, Mac." Morgan's voice rang in his ear. His business partner's drawl spoke of the Deep South, unlike Les' honey-toned accent.

"Morgan. How's things going?" He walked away for privacy.

"Good. I need to get a few figures from you on the Aaron job. She's interested in installing one of our systems and hiring one of our guys. Her accountant wants the numbers." A rustle of paper let Brody know his partner was at the office.

"Give me ten minutes and I'll call you back. I'm not near my laptop."

"Sure. As long as you get back to me sometime today."

"I will. Bye." He hung up.

When he returned to Les' side, Tony and Randy were still rolling around. He nudged Les. "If we pour water on them, it would be like mud wrestling."

"A wet T-shirt contest, huh?" Les' dark eyes twinkled. "While I'm not opposed to seeing Randy wet, I think it's a little too cold at the moment."

"Damn. Guess I'll have to wait until summer for that." His whistle was shrill, stopping the two men cold. "Hey, sweet cheeks, I need to go in for a while."

Randy's mouth dropped open and Tony's face flushed red. Both of them stared at each other before Randy looked at him.

"Um-m-m...okay."

Brody chuckled. "While I'm sure your ass is sweet, it wasn't you I was talking to." He gestured to Tony. "It was the short one."

"You better start running," Les told him under his breath.

He winked, spun on his heel then ran from the arena. Looking back over his shoulder, he saw Les grab Tony and stop the bull rider from chasing him. Brody had a feeling he would pay for the short comment, and maybe the 'sweet cheeks' as well.

* * * *

"Tony, stop teasing," Brody moaned.

Tony glanced up from where he was kneeling between Brody's legs and grinned. He'd been plotting his revenge all during supper and watching movies with the others. He pumped his hand up and down over Brody's cock, making sure his grip was tight. Licking along the throbbing vein on the underside of Brody's shaft, he savoured the salty taste of Brody's skin.

Brody's hips surged off the edge of the bed. Tony pinned him down with one hand and shook his head. Pulling off Brody's cock with a soft pop, he glared at the man.

"No moving."

A pout pushed Brody's bottom lip out. "You've been sucking me for twenty minutes now, but you won't let me come. Are you getting back at me for the short remark earlier?"

"Oh, no. I'd never be that vindictive." He leered at his lover. "I simply love sucking your cock." He stroked the thick shaft in his fist, twisting his palm over the crown.

"Let go of my dick before lightning strikes you." Brody flopped back on the bed and sighed. He waved a hand at Tony. "Get on with it. I might die before you let me come."

"Poor thing. It could be an interesting way to go." He flicked his tongue over the spongy head in his hand.

Brody twitched then stilled. "How would Yancey explain that to my father? Brody died because the guy sucking his cock wouldn't let him come."

Tony burst out laughing. "You're right. Doesn't look good in the obituary."

Taking pity on Brody, he leant forward and swallowed Brody's cock down to its base.

"Fuck." Brody's voice was low and harsh.

Tony hummed his approval, allowing Brody to move in and out of his mouth. He slid one finger in along with Brody's cock, making it as wet. He eased his finger down behind Brody's balls to where Brody's puckered opening hid. Pressing the tip of his finger against Brody's hole, he let Brody slowly begin to fuck himself on it. Tony didn't try to push farther into Brody's ass.

Groaning, Brody reached down and wrapped a hand around one muscled thigh. He lifted the leg up and out, displaying the stretched ring of muscles to Tony's gaze. Tony's cock ached. He wanted to be buried deep inside Brody when his lover came. One finger became two and he managed to nail Brody's gland with the second thrust.

"Tony." Brody twisted his hands in the sheets.

Tony moved away, reaching for the lube and a condom. Brody protested, rolling his hips to entice Tony back. Tony ripped open the foil package then slid the latex on his cock. After squirting some lube on his hand, he covered the rubber before crawling on to the bed.

Brody moved farther up the mattress, settling against the pillows. Tony hooked Brody's thighs over his arms and pressed the head of his cock into Brody's ass. He rocked back and forth, each push going in deeper than the one before, until his balls slapped

Brody. Brody braced his hands on the headboard and matched Tony thrust for thrust.

"Shit, Brody. I love your ass." Tony grunted, slamming into Brody faster and harder.

Brody seemed beyond words, his blue eyes rolling as his inner channel clamped down on Tony's shaft, squeezing him. Cum exploded out of Brody's cock, covering their stomachs and chests. Tony tightened his grip on Brody's thighs and reamed his lover. His balls drew up as his climax burst over him, filling the condom.

He dropped Brody's thighs and collapsed on top of the man. Brody threaded his hands through Tony's hair and stroked the nape of his neck. Tony waited until his breathing had calmed before he rolled to the side.

They groaned as his softened cock slid out of Brody's ass. Tony stared up at the ceiling, trying to decide whether he had enough strength to get up and clean off. Brody climbed out of bed and headed to the bathroom. Tony closed his eyes while Brody took care of the rubber and washed him as well.

Brody eased back in bed and Tony snuggled with his lover. After Brody had stopped fidgeting for a while, Tony thought Brody had fallen asleep, and he was surprised when Brody spoke.

"I have to head back to L.A. tomorrow."

Tony braced himself on an elbow and stared down at Brody. "I thought you were going to stay a couple more days."

"I was, but Morgan said this new client wants to meet with all of us about her security. Not only does she want a bodyguard, she wants a security system as well." Brody sighed. "The systems were my idea. I'm the one who knows the most about them. I need to be there to seal the deal."

Disappointment shot through Tony. He'd hoped to have more time with Brody before they went back to their regular lives. "I understand."

It was true. He did understand having to do what he needed to make a living. It was why he spent most of his time and sacrificed most of his weekends travelling to events throughout the country.

Brody reached up and cupped his cheek, regret glowing in his blue eyes. "I'm sorry. Does the PBR come to California?"

He perked up. "Yeah. There's several events in California. I just got done with two. Maybe we can hook up when I come to compete? I'll check the schedule and let you know when we'll be there."

"I'll make sure to clear my calendar." Brody closed his eyes and took a breath. When he met Tony's eyes again, he looked serious. "I want to try and make this work, Tony. Silly, isn't it? We've had a one-night stand and then somehow managed to find each other again."

"We're getting sappy here," Tony teased. "I thought about you a lot after I got back from Hawaii. As strange as it may sound, I feel there's a connection between us and I'd like to explore it a little more."

"I can rearrange things so I'm flexible. Maybe I'll hit a couple events with you." Brody winked. "I'd like to see you compete."

"I'm a stud." He grinned.

"Yes, you are."

Brody pulled his head down to kiss him and Tony stopped worrying about what was going to happen tomorrow.

Chapter Eleven

Three weeks later, Los Angeles, California

"I head out to St Louis tomorrow. Did you want to come with me?" Tony checked his bull rope, making sure there weren't any frays or broken strands.

Brody glanced up, surprise shining in his eyes. "Really? I enjoyed watching you in Anaheim. I'll try to remember the rules, but won't the guys start wondering if I show up at several events with you?"

He frowned. "No one'll say a word. Randy and Les have come to see me compete several times."

Brody nodded. "Makes sense. I'd like that. I'm becoming addicted to watching you." A wicked gleam twinkled in his eyes. "I know how well you ride me."

Tony threw his riding glove at his lover. "Perv. You're not supposed to have those types of thoughts when you're watching bull riding."

"I'm not? Shit. Wish someone had said something." Brody grinned. "What the hell am I supposed to think? All those tight-assed cowboys rocking their hips like that? It's every gay man's wet dream."

Tony looked to see Brody standing in front of him, the man's groin level with his mouth. Shooting Brody a smirk, he leant forward and blew a puff of hot air over the bulge behind Brody's zipper.

"Fuck." Brody's hips jerked, but he pulled away before Tony could go further.

Brody sat on the arm of Tony's chair. "So where did you say we're heading to this weekend?"

"St Louis." He folded his rope and packed it back in his bag.

"Missouri? Not really the first place I'd think of when it comes to riding bulls."

"The PBR is getting bigger every year. Seems like we're adding new venues all the time. This year we're having a world event in Queensland, Australia." Tony leant back in the chair, resting his hand on Brody's thigh.

"You going to that? My passport's up-to-date." Brody's hand settled over his, a warm solid presence.

"I started late this year and missed a couple of events getting things worked out with Juan. I need to dig in and start riding if I want enough points to win the championship."

Tony had injured his right shoulder in the middle part of last year, making it difficult to shine during his rookie season on tour. By the time it'd healed enough for the doctors to let him compete, he'd missed the first two events of this year.

He'd finished second in Fresno and third in Sacramento. But then Juan had come and he'd stayed home to help his nephew settle in. He'd won the Anaheim event, so he was getting back into form.

"You coming with me?" He looked up at Brody.

Brody shrugged. "Sure. Morgan and Vance can run the main company without me for the most part. I have some meetings set up to talk about installing security systems, but those aren't until next week. I can fly back for those."

"Who knew such a pretty face hid the brain of a business genius," he teased.

"I didn't." Yancey wandered in, dropping down on the couch. "Though being a bodyguard is a career path I'm not surprised you took."

Brody's younger brother had been out visiting for a week or so but Tony knew Yancey was planning on heading back to Wyoming soon.

"Like beating up on people, huh?" Tony let his hand slide down to trace the seam of Brody's jeans, right below his groin.

"Beating up people is just a perk of the job. I like protecting people and some of them are pretty nice. I did some work for Derek St Martin." Brody shifted and Tony wasn't sure if he was trying to get Tony to touch him harder or moving away from him.

"Really? What was he like?" Yancey slid down until he was lying on the couch.

"Nice guy. Didn't act like an asshole or anything. When they get to be as famous as he is, you come to expect being treated like shit, but he didn't do that." A crease formed between Brody's eyebrows. "I don't think he's happy, though."

"Why do you say that?"

Tony bit his tongue. He'd never told anyone about his flight home from Honolulu. Figured it wasn't anyone's business and he wasn't about to out the singer.

"Don't know. It's more of a feeling. The only time he seems really happy is when he's singing. There were times when I'd hear him get up in the middle of the night. I'd go check on him and he'd be curled up in a chair in the dark, playing his guitar and singing. The songs he sang would bring tears to my eyes." Brody closed his eyes and a soft smile graced his face. "His sales would go through the roof if he released some of those."

"What does he have to be unhappy about?" Yancey waved his hand in the air. "He has money. His face is on every fucking magazine cover in the world."

"Yancey," Brody warned.

"Sorry. He can have anything he wants. What does he have to be unhappy about?" Yancey sounded confused.

"Maybe he's got a secret and can't tell anyone what it is." Tony wanted to hit himself in the head. He ducked his head. Shit, he really needed to learn how to keep his mouth shut.

"Sounds like you have an idea of what his secret might be." Brody tapped him on the top of his head.

He denied it. "No. Just a guess."

"Uh-huh." Brody didn't sound convinced. "I was in Hawaii, working for St Martin when we met. He flew out the same day you did and from what I heard, he slipped his entourage and took a commercial jet to San Fran. Thank God, my company wasn't on duty that day."

"I'm thirsty. Who wants a drink?" Tony shot to his feet, managing to dodge Brody's hand, and headed for the kitchen.

"Get back here. I think you're hiding something." Brody snagged the waistband of Tony's jeans, not letting him get away. "It seems to me you flew back at the same time St Martin did. I wonder if you saw him?"

He bit his lip and studied the floor for a second. Looking up, he met Brody's gaze before looking at

Yancey. "I know I can trust both of you not to say anything. I don't want to hurt him with rumours, even though he outed himself to me pretty much from the moment I met him."

"You met Derek St Martin?" Yancey's mouth fell open. "And you're saying he's gay?"

Tony nodded. "Yeah. I got the feeling he's been hiding it and it's wearing on him. When he runs away, it's his way of finding some freedom once in a while."

Brody looked thoughtful. "I can see why being a country star would be hard for him."

"Being any kind of star is hard, but can you imagine having to hide it? There can't be a hint of him being gay." Tony packed his rope away, making sure the bell wouldn't rub on the hemp.

Silence reigned for a few moments before Brody shook himself and smiled.

"I think we should go out tonight. Do a little dancing. I haven't had a chance to show either of you L.A. night life. It won't be really busy, since it's a week night."

"Awesome." Yancey jumped to his feet and raced down the hallway to the room Brody had given him. "I'll be ready in a few."

Tony laughed. "Oh, to be young again."

"I don't want to be young again. I'm happy right where I am." Brody wrapped his arms around Tony's waist and pulled him tight to him.

He rested his hands on Brody's shoulders and rose on his toes to brush a kiss over Brody's lips. "So am I."

"Let's change. I can't wait to dance with you." Brody's low voice caused shivers to race over Tony's body.

"Considering how well you make love, I'm betting you're a great dancer." He ground his groin into Brody's.

"It's all in the hips." Brody squeezed Tony's ass.

"M-m-m…" He hummed softly. "We should go change as well. Don't want the kid to show us up."

Laughing, Brody kissed him quickly then stepped away. "I don't think we have to worry about that."

He followed Brody to their bedroom. He was looking forward to dancing and spending time with Brody without having to worry about who might be watching them.

* * * *

Brody waited for the bartender to get him two beers. Turning, he leant back and rested his elbow on the bar. He smiled when he caught sight of Yancey and Tony dancing. He reached down and adjusted his cock, trying to find room in his jeans. He should have known Tony would be a great dancer. A man had to have a certain sense of rhythm to ride bulls. His brother was matching Tony step for step.

"Delicious."

He turned to see two men standing next to him at the bar. They were studying his lover and his brother. Lust burned on their faces and in their voices.

"Do you suppose they belong to each other?"

"I don't know, but I think I'll go and find out."

He wanted to stop them and tell them not to go, but he knew Tony could handle himself and Yancey wasn't interested in picking up guys anymore. Part of that had to do with Juan and part of it was simply the fact his brother didn't need to turn tricks anymore to survive.

"Here you go, Brody." The bartender set the bottles on the bar. A wink shot his way. "I see the barflies have spotted your guy."

"Yeah, but Tony can take care of himself. I'm not worried about it." He handed the money over and grabbed the beer. "Thanks."

He headed back to the booth they had grabbed as soon as they'd got to the club. The bouncer knew Brody and had let Yancey in because he knew Brody wouldn't allow his brother to drink. Settling down in the booth, he sipped the beer and watched the barflies get shot down by his companions.

The music slowed down and Tony glanced over at him. He didn't dance, but he couldn't resist holding that compact hard body tight to his own. He eased through the crowd to where Tony stood.

"May I have this dance?" He smiled, holding his arms open.

"Oh, yes." Tony walked into his embrace, wrapping his arms around Brody's shoulders.

Brody checked on Yancey and saw his brother dancing with an auburn-haired man in a suit. Brody caught Yancey's eye and nodded. His brother grinned back.

"He can take care of himself." Tony tugged on Brody's hair to bring his attention back.

"I know. I just wanted to let him know the guy was okay. I've danced with him a few times. He's a nice guy. Sort of quiet, though." He hugged Tony tighter to him.

Their erections brushed against each other and Tony's sigh brushed over Brody's chin.

"Did you sleep with him?" Tony's question was low.

Brody chuckled. "Does it matter if I did? I'm not sleeping with him now."

"No. I was just curious how you knew he was quiet."

He pinched Tony's ass and the bull rider squeaked. "Same way I know I like my lovers noisy and pushy."

"Ass," Tony muttered.

He nuzzled Tony's dark curls, cupping Tony's firm cheeks with his hands. He eased his thigh between Tony's legs and rocked their groins together in time with the music.

Tony gasped. "If you keep doing that, I'm going to cream my jeans and I'm not going to be happy about dancing in wet pants all night."

"Who said we had to close down the club?" He sucked on Tony's earlobe, causing the man to arch and hump his leg faster.

"You're evil." Tony pushed him away, dark eyes flashing and olive skin flushed. "Take me home and fuck me, Brody."

He swallowed, his mouth suddenly dry. Glancing around, he found Yancey standing at the edge of the dance floor talking to Morgan. He grabbed Tony's hand, dragging him along as he headed over there.

"Yancey, Tony and I are heading back to my place. If you want to hang here for a while, I'm sure Morgan would be willing to give you a ride home."

His brother looked at him and with a knowing smile, nodded. "Sure. As long as Morgan doesn't have a problem with getting stuck with me."

Morgan swung a thick arm around Yancey's shoulder and laughed. "No problem. I'll probably have to beat the guys off with a stick. You two get out of here before you set the sprinklers off."

Brody felt his cheeks heat. Okay, so it was obvious what they were going to do, but he didn't care. All he wanted was to bury his cock in Tony's ass as soon as possible.

"Fuck you, Kozlov. See you later, Yancey."

They didn't wait to hear Yancey's goodbye.

* * * *

Brody managed to keep them from hitting the floor as they fell into the apartment. Getting the door shut and locked was a major feat with Tony wrapped around him like an octopus. The fact they were back inside the apartment must have registered in Tony's brain because his lover dropped to his knees and started unfastening Brody's pants.

"Fuck." His head slammed back against the door when Tony swallowed his cock down to the root.

He buried his fingers into Tony's curls, trying not to pull on them as Tony licked up and down his shaft. He trailed one hand down to feel his lover's stubble-covered cheeks hollow with each suck.

Brody had been on the edge since the club and he knew it would take no time at all for Tony to make him come. His balls drew up and the small of his back tingled. He tugged lightly at Tony's head.

Tony came off him with a pop and wiped his mouth as he eased back on his heels. Those burning dark eyes met his.

"I want to be in you when I come and I'm close." Brody gripped the base of his cock tightly. "Go get ready. If I help you or watch you, this will be over."

His lover sprang to his feet and raced to the bedroom. Brody chuckled. It had been some time since he'd had a lover as eager as Tony. He got him hot and bothered faster than any other lover had. He stripped, leaving a trail of clothes throughout the apartment leading to his bedroom. Stopping outside the bedroom door, he thought about how he felt when he was around Tony.

Maybe it wasn't so much that Tony was eager to have sex that turned him on, as it was Tony wanting to have sex with him so badly. His other partners had loved sex, but it didn't matter who they were having it with. Brody rested his head against the doorframe.

Unrelenting desire, need and attraction combined with the fact that he liked Tony made this relationship one he was willing to work at keeping.

"Where the fuck are you, MacCafferty? You better get your ass in here."

Tony's shouted demand made Brody smile and push into the bedroom.

Tony was sprawled on the bed, his hands hooked behind his knees, spreading them for Brody. Lube and condoms were next to him. His gaze trailed over Brody's body, leaving what felt like scorch marks where his gaze rested.

Without saying a word, he opened the foil package and slipped the rubber on his cock. He popped the top of the lube, squirting some in his palm. After tossing the tube to the side, he smeared the lube over his shaft then joined Tony on the bed.

After crawling up the mattress, he placed Tony's legs over his shoulder and positioned the head of his cock at Tony's hole. He rubbed it over the sensitive pucker.

Tony snarled. "Take me, Brody. Don't tease."

He eased an inch in and Tony hissed. Waiting for a moment, he reached out and pinched one of Tony's nipples.

The bull rider's hips lifted off the sheet. Brody thrust in, not stopping this time until he was as deep in Tony's ass as he thought he could be.

"Wait." Tony fisted the sheets beneath him.

Brody froze. The signal to move came a few seconds later when Tony rocked against him and took him an inch deeper.

"Now."

He didn't hesitate after that. He drove into Tony's ass, taking his lover hard and fast like Tony wanted. Brody knew his grip would leave bruises on Tony's hips, but he didn't care. In a small part of his mind, he wanted to mark Tony, so if anyone noticed, they would know Tony had a lover.

Brody changed the angle of his thrusts.

"There." Tony pushed back on his cock.

Grunting, Brody made sure to nail that spot every stroke in. Tony's inner channel spasmed around him, milking him, encouraging him to come.

"Touch yourself," he ordered.

Tony pumped his cock, twisting his hand around the shaft. Brody groaned and watched Tony press his thumb into his slit. Tony sat up slightly and slid his other hand down between them. He ran his fingers over his stretched opening and his rough calluses caught on Brody's cock, driving shocks of desire to his balls.

"Shit."

Brody's eyes crossed when Tony clasped almost too tightly around his shaft. Pearly ropes of cum shot from Tony's cock, splashing over their chests and Tony's hand. Brody kept moving, riding through Tony's climax. When the last drop landed, Tony opened his eyes and met Brody's gaze.

He held his breath as Tony lifted his cum-covered hand to his mouth and started licking his hand clean.

"So fucking sexy," Brody swore and slammed into Tony, filling the condom with his spunk.

His strength deserted him after his climax faded. He crumpled to the side, making sure not to fall on Tony. He threw an arm over his eyes and let himself slip towards sleep.

"Poor baby. Did I wear you out?" Tony trailed his hand over his chest and dipped his finger into his belly button.

"Yes. You did. Now let me rest for a second before I have to get up and clean off." He swatted at Tony's hand.

He heard Tony chuckle. The condom was eased off his limp cock. He must have drifted off to sleep because he didn't hear Tony leave the bed. He woke up when Tony washed him with a warm, wet cloth. He reached out and patted Tony's shoulder.

"Thank you."

Tony cuddled close, throwing a leg over his and covering them with the blankets. A kiss brushed over his chest. "You're welcome."

Brody held Tony close as he went back to sleep.

Chapter Twelve

Enterprise Rent-a-Car Classic, St Louis, Missouri

"Hey, Tony."

Brody and Tony turned when they heard Tony's name shouted. A young blond cowboy came running up to them. He thumped Tony on the back.

"Wasn't sure if I'd see you here." The kid nodded at Brody with a friendly smile.

"Sorry, Cody. Had some personal stuff to take care of. Wasn't competing regular enough to travel with you." Tony grinned at Cody. "This is my friend, Brody MacCafferty. Brody, this is Cody Harwood. He was my travelling partner last year."

Brody shook the kid's hand, liking the firm grip. "Nice meeting you."

"You too." Cody pointed to the area behind the bull chutes. "Almost time for the show to start."

"Yeah. I'll meet you back there." Tony waited for Cody to move off before he turned to look at Brody. "You know where your seat is, right?"

"Don't worry. I can find it." Brody squeezed Tony's shoulder. He fought the urge to give Tony a kiss for good luck. "I'll meet you out by the car when this is over."

"Good. Maybe we'll have something to celebrate." Tony winked then walked away.

Brody sighed, trying not to get caught watching Tony's ass. When his lover had disappeared around the corner, he went to find his seat.

An hour later, Brody looked down at the programme. Tony's friend, Cody Harwood, was up next.

"Poor kid's got Tank's Reward," the woman sitting next to Brody commented. She must have caught sight of his puzzled frown. "Tank's Reward is the highest-rated bull on tour. His buck-off time is two-point-three seconds."

"What's that mean?"

She smiled at him. "First time?"

"No. I'm a friend of Tony Romanos and I've seen him ride a few times, but I still don't understand everything."

"Romanos is doing great this year." The woman laughed. "Buck-off time is how long it takes the bull to buck the cowboys off. Tank's been out five times this year. Never been ridden. Most cowboys don't make it past the first jump out of the gate with him."

Brody looked at where she pointed. A large, black bull stood in chute three. He saw Tony standing behind the chute on a platform. A guy sat on the bull's back, adjusting a rope.

"Tank's dangerous. He's got a lot of power, which is what gets the riders off centre." The woman scooted closer to Brody. "See, the thing is, everyone knows the bull jumps from the chute and always goes to the right for the first spin, but it's the explosion out of the gate that gets them." She waved to someone in the seats below them. "Tank's big and strong. He drives the cowboys off their ropes and that's all she wrote. He spins and they drop into the well."

"The well?"

"When the bull spins, he creates what the riders call the well. It's the space on the inside of the spin. The more the bull spins, the more force is put on the rider to fall into that space or well. It also can be one of the worst places for a rider to fall. He can get hit by the bull's horns or head." The lady seemed willing to share her knowledge with him.

"What makes him so dangerous?" Brody noticed Tony looking up at him. He nodded and Tony's quick grin caused his cock to stiffen. He hoped the woman didn't notice.

"Once he has a rider down, he does his level best to kill him. Tank steps on them, tries to gore or hook them." She gestured to Cody refastening his vest. "Several guys have been thankful for those vests. If the bull's in a mood, it'll take the rider roping him and dragging him back to the pen before he leaves the arena. Tank's gonna kill someone one of these days." She settled back, eyes focused on the arena floor.

Brody felt his stomach flutter, glad Tony hadn't drawn that bull. He watched Tony slap Cody on the shoulder then step back. Cody pushed his cowboy hat down, crept up tight to where he held his bull rope and nodded. The gate man yanked open the chute and Brody got to see what the woman was talking about.

The large bull exploded from the chute like a demon escaping hell. Brody swore the ground shook when the beast's front hooves landed. His back feet cleared the top of the gate and Brody knew Cody was in trouble. The kid jerked forward as Tank flung his head back.

Right spin and Cody fell into the well, unconscious. Brody jumped to his feet as Cody dangled from the back of the monster, feet dragging the ground. The bullfighters were trying desperately to get Cody's hand free of the rope, but Tank wasn't letting any man close to him.

Brody winced when he saw the animal step on Cody's leg. It had to be broken. Cody's limp body was flung left and right like a rag doll being tossed by a child. Brody shot a glance over to see Tony perched on the gate, ready to leap into the arena. He wanted to shout at his lover, but knew even if Tony could hear him, it wouldn't stop the man from trying to save Cody's life.

Tank chased one of the bullfighters to the fence. The man climbed to the top rail, avoiding the bull's horns. Tank swerved, pinning Cody between his body and the fence. That allowed the other bullfighters to jerk on the tail of the rope, freeing Cody's hand. The third fighter got Tank to follow him, leaving behind the broken and bloodied Cody. Tony was in the arena and racing towards Cody the minute the cowboy's body hit the dirt. Brody clenched his hands and stuffed them in his pockets. Anything to hide the trembling.

The black bull stopped in the middle of the arena. Its head was held high and Brody could imagine he was surveying the destruction he'd wrought. The silence was deafening. No one moved. In a weird way, it was like all the people that night existed merely as secondary characters to the main star. Tank's Reward snorted.

"Get the medics out here now," Tony yelled.

The tableau broke and the demon's head snapped around. Brody wondered if the bull understood what Tony had said, but more than likely the beast knew men on two legs posed no threat to him.

"Fuck," Brody whispered as Tank's Reward spun around and charged the two vulnerable men huddled on the dirt.

Tony hunched over Cody's prone body. He would do everything he could to protect his friend. The ground shook with each stride the charging hamburger took. Tony didn't have his vest on so things could go badly if he caught a horn.

A gasp rose from the crowd. Peeking from under his arm, he saw one of the bullfighters go cartwheeling through the air. Tony held his breath, waiting for the man to hit the ground. Amazingly, he managed to land on his feet and keep running. Another of the fighters threw his hat into the bull's face. Tank tilted his head, trying to hook the straw creation. Tony drew a breath as Tank got closer. Nothing the other men did distracted the bull from his target. He braced to catch a horn or get kicked by a hoof.

Hot air bathed him when an explosive grunt sounded a few feet away from him. Glancing up, he saw a mounted rider driving Tank back. The man must have ridden his horse into Tank's side, forcing the bull to move away. He heard the rattling groan as Cody tried to breathe.

Tony swallowed, staring down at the blood-covered face of his friend. Cody wasn't recognisable. There was so much blood and damage to his face alone. He didn't know what other injuries Cody might have sustained having been flung around like he had been.

The doctors skidded to a halt and dropped next to him. They pushed him out of the way while they worked to stabilise Cody. A brace was wrapped around Cody's neck to keep from causing any more damage to the man's back. He helped them put his friend on a stretcher and it was only as he was running out of the arena, following the EMTs that he thought about Brody.

He glanced up into the stands. Brody was standing up and making his way to the aisle. They looked at each other and Brody nodded. His lover understood he was going to the hospital with his friend.

'Meet you there,' Brody mouthed at him.

He grinned feebly.

* * * *

Tony gripped his knees. Waiting to hear about Cody was difficult. He jumped to his feet and started to pace. Brody sat quiet and still. Tony couldn't understand how his lover could be so calm. A phone rang and Brody pulled his own cell phone out of his pocket.

Tony's hands shook. God, he wanted a smoke, but he didn't want to risk missing the doctor if the man came looking for him. He pointed to the hall. He'd go out there. His restlessness was probably annoying the other people in the room.

Still on the phone, Brody followed him out. He focused on Brody's conversation.

"St Martin again?" Brody's blue eyes focused on Tony.

He managed a slight smile. His nerves were getting the best of him, but he wasn't falling apart yet. Cody had been a good friend and travelling partner. He was one of the few riders who knew Tony was gay. Cody had been surprised at first, but hadn't allowed it to ruin their friendship. Tony rarely allowed people close, so when he did, he hated to see them hurt.

"I can't. I don't care if he requested me, Morgan." Brody trailed his hand over Tony's arm as he paced past where his lover leaned against the wall, phone pressed to his ear. "Send Joe. He's a good guy. One of our best. Calm and easy-going."

A pause.

"He has to be. St Martin's wired so tight, he needs someone to talk him down." Brody gave Tony a quick wink.

Tony remembered his own meeting with the country singer. It was true. Derek St Martin was a powder keg waiting to explode. It would take a really laid-back person to deal with him.

"Mr Romanos?" A short, thin man dressed in scrubs stepped into the hall.

"That's me." Tony rubbed his palm on his jeans before shaking the doctor's hand.

"Morgan, I have to go. I'll talk to you tomorrow." Brody ended the call, stuffing his phone back in a pocket.

The heat from Brody's body surrounded Tony as his lover came to stand behind him. Relief flowed through him. It was nice to have someone around to hold on to if he needed.

"How's Cody?" Tony didn't like the serious expression on the doctor's face.

"We're not sure. Mr Harwood has been stabilised and sedated. His collarbone's broken, along with several ribs and his right leg. There's no internal bleeding, which is a good sign." The doctor rubbed his tired-looking eyes. "We think he's broken his neck, but we can't be completely sure until the swelling goes down."

Tony bit back a moan. A broken neck. No one ever wanted to hear that.

"What about his face?" Brody asked, giving Tony a chance to recover.

"That's another issue we won't know the total extent of until we get the swelling down, though I do believe he'll need extensive plastic surgery to rebuild much of his face. As far as we can tell, a majority of the bones were crushed when he made contact with the top of the animal's head."

A nurse handed the doctor some papers. He flipped through them and said, "Mr Harwood is being moved up to ICU now. You might as well go back to your hotel. He won't be awake until later tomorrow, I believe."

"Thank you, Doctor." Brody shook the man's hand.

Tony was in shock. What would Cody do if he couldn't ride? Being part of the PBR had been his friend's dream since he could talk.

"We have your phone number. The nurses will contact you if there's any change." The doctor nodded and left.

Brody put a hand on the small of Tony's back, guiding him out of the hospital. Tony couldn't make his mind work. Before the doctor's report, he'd believed Cody would be okay. Maybe suffer a concussion and have to sit out a couple of events. These injuries were more serious than that.

He stopped long enough to light a cigarette. The first drag burned his lungs and he held the smoke in for a second. Blowing it out, he felt his nerves settle slightly.

"Let's go to the hotel and clean you up. We'll worry about calling whoever we have to call later." Brody grasped his hand.

He held tight to his lover's large hand. The feel of solid flesh and a strong grip helped keep him grounded. How was he going to tell Cody's parents?

* * * *

An hour later, Brody sat next to Tony. He'd got his cowboy showered and cleaned up. Tony wore a pair of white boxer-briefs now, his dark hair still damp from the shower. A shudder racked Tony's muscular body and Brody knew what he had to do. Stripping, he climbed on the bed, leaned against the headboard and tugged Tony into his arms. Trembling, Tony curled up on his lap. He ran his hands over Tony's back. Brody knew how much touch helped in a situation like this.

No words were spoken. He continued to hold Tony until his lover fell asleep. He eased out from under Tony's warm body and tucked the blanket around him. Before he'd showered, Tony had insisted on calling Cody's parents. From Tony's side of the conversation, the couple would be driving in tomorrow.

Tony's phone rang and Brody searched through their bags quickly to find it. He checked the ID and answered before the ringing woke Tony.

"Hey, Les." He pulled on a pair of jeans and stepped out onto the balcony, leaving the sliding door open.

"Brody." If Les was surprised that Brody answered Tony's phone, he didn't sound it. "Is Tony around?"

"He's sleeping." Brody stared out over the skyline. It was moments like these when he wished he still smoked.

"Really? I was calling to see how he did today."

"Ah, fuck. We'll have to find out tomorrow. We left the arena before the round was finished." He rested his elbows on the railing, rubbing the back of his neck.

"Why? Is Tony all right?" Les' concern filled his honey-toned voice.

"He'll be fine. His friend, Cody Harwood, was in a nasty wreck today. We went with him to the hospital." He sighed. "Broken collarbone, ribs and leg. The doctors think he might have broken his neck as well, but won't know until the swelling's down. They have him sedated. His face is smashed. I see a lot of reconstructive surgery for that."

"Poor kid. What can we do for him?"

One of the many things Brody liked about Les was the man's willingness to help anyone who needed it. Many people believed that part of his personality stemmed from his own accident, but Brody had the feeling Les had always been giving.

"At the moment, I don't know. The medical bills are going to be huge, especially if he did break his neck."

A glimmer of an idea started forming in his mind and Les was the man to talk to about it.

"I've only gone to a couple events so far, but it seems to me that it's really fucking dangerous. Guys get injured every night and some seriously."

"Both Randy and Tony have tried to explain to me the fact that danger is one of the beauties of the sport. I've never understood the rough stock events. Maybe they're right and the danger is what makes them so popular."

"The medical bills have got to be a burden for some of those guys. What if there was a fund set up to help defray those costs?" Brody shut his eyes, running numbers in his mind.

"There probably is something like that, but it never hurts to have more fall-back funds." Les' voice was thoughtful. "I'll have Peter look into it."

"I'm willing to donate money to start it," Brody said. "I'm thinking about how hard Tony had to work to afford entry fees and gas money to get to the events. Maybe sponsoring a new rider would work as well." He was thinking out loud now.

"We'll look into it."

He heard a rustling noise and figured Les was writing something down.

"How's Randy and the boys?"

Les' chuckle washed over him, easing tension Brody hadn't even known he'd had.

"Yancey and Juan are fine. Jackson has both of them helping with the horses. Though I think Juan seems more interested in the jumpers than he does the cutting horses." Les snorted. "Randy has decided that neither of us has enough to do, so he's going to work on setting up riding lessons for area kids."

"I think he has too much energy. You need to have more sex and wear the guy out." Brody grinned, imagining Randy's usual boundless store of energy.

"We get enough comments from the guys around here about our sex life already. You know Tony's the same way when he's not riding. Picture what you have to look forward to when the season is over with."

Brody groaned. "I don't know if I'll be able to survive."

They laughed together. Brody let silence reign for a moment before he continued in a causal tone.

"I was wondering if you could do me a favour, Hardin?"

"Sure. Anything."

Les' reply was exactly what Brody had figured the man would say.

"I'm looking to buy a ranch."

"Been bit by the bug, huh?"

"Well, not really, but Yancey likes Wyoming and I know Tony would like to stay near you and Randy." Brody waited.

"You serious?" Les' question was low.

"Yes, I am." He closed his eyes. "I know Tony and I haven't been together for long, but there's something between us. I'm willing to relocate to find out if it'll last. It's not like I have anything to hold me in L.A.."

"How's Tony feel about it?"

"He doesn't know I'm looking. I know he feels the same way I do about our relationship."

"What about your company?" Les didn't seem inclined to talk him out of it.

"I can run it from the ranch. Morgan and Vance can take over more of the daily running. I'll have to travel for the security systems stuff, but once a month face-to-face meetings and it'll work." He sighed. "I wasn't around for five years of Yancey's life. Five years when he needed me. I don't want to do that again."

"Understandable. I'll have the real estate agent I worked with start looking for you. Maybe she can find something close by."

"That would be great. Thanks, Les." He yawned.

"You're welcome. Run off to bed. Give Tony a hug from us and tell him to call us tomorrow."

"Will do." Brody ended the call.

He stood, breathing in the crisp night air, before heading back inside. His jeans landed in a pile next to the suitcase. Tony mumbled something when Brody slid into bed next to him, but didn't wake up. He slipped an arm around Tony's narrow waist, spooning tightly with his lover. He fell asleep with the warm scent of Tony in his nose.

Chapter Thirteen

Two days later

Tony swallowed and straightened his shoulders. This was going to be one of the hardest things he'd ever done. He stuffed his hands in his pockets. It didn't help because they kept shaking.

Cody's parents had called him as he and Brody were leaving the hotel to let him know Cody could finally have visitors. The cowboy was still groggy and pretty out of it, but Tony needed to see him before he headed back to Wyoming.

He jumped when Brody wrapped an arm around his waist and pulled him in for a tight hug. He relaxed, knowing Brody would hold him. Brody kissed his cheek quickly.

"It'll be all right," Brody whispered in his ear. "I'll be out here waiting."

Tony nodded. Knowing Brody waited for him was the only way he could get through this. He stepped away from his lover and pushed open the door.

Cody's parents looked up from their spots at his bedside. Mr Harwood stood, offering Tony his hand. Tony shook it, recognising the rough grip and weathered skin of a farmer. Cody's parents owned a small farm in the southwest part of Missouri. Mrs Harwood stood and hugged him.

"He can't talk and he tends to fade in and out, but he does know when someone is here." She leaned over the bed railing and brushed a limp curl off Cody's forehead. "Cody, honey. Your friend Tony is here."

Cody's eyes didn't open, but he shifted like he was acknowledging his mother's words.

"We'll be outside. I'm afraid you can only stay ten minutes." Mr Harwood ushered his wife towards the door.

"That's okay. I have to head home today anyway." He went to take the chair Cody's father had been sitting in.

"Tell him about the round yesterday. I know he'll want to know if you won or not." Cody's mother smiled at him, a tired look in her eyes.

"I will, ma'am."

He sat, resting his hands on his knees. He forced himself to look at Cody. His friend's face was so swollen there were no distinguishable features. Cody's breath rattled through a tube inserted in his throat. There wasn't any other way for Cody to get air into his lungs at the moment.

Reaching over the bed railing, Tony took Cody's hand in his. He gave it a slight squeeze. He almost fell out of the chair when he got a corresponding one back.

"Are you with me, Cody?" He kept his voice low.

Another squeeze. For a moment, he was at a loss. Did Cody really want to know the results of the event?

"You want to know who won?"

A harder squeeze this time. He chuckled. Just like a bull rider. Nothing mattered except who rode and who didn't. He settled back, keeping Cody's hand in his and started telling his friend about the scores.

"I didn't win. Bucked off the money bull. Fucking easiest bull in the pen and I let him toss me off like garbage."

Ten minutes later, his throat was dry. He'd been talking continuously. He looked up as the door eased open. Mr and Mrs Harwood entered. He squeezed Cody's hand and let it go.

"Time for me to go, Cody. Take it easy, man, and I'll check up on you." He winked at Mrs Harwood. "I'll make sure your mother gets a play-by-play of the events to tell you. Have to keep up on the competition."

"Thank you, Tony." Mrs Harwood gave him a quick hug before she hurried over to check on Cody.

Mr Harwood and Tony went out in the hall. Brody stood from where he'd been sitting against the wall across from the door. Tony smiled at his lover before turning to say goodbye to Cody's dad.

"Your friend tells me we don't have to worry about Cody's bills." Mr Harwood nodded towards Brody.

Tony shot a surprised look in Brody's direction. Butter wouldn't have melted in the man's mouth, judging by the innocent expression on his face.

"If Brody told you that, Mr Harwood, it has to be true." Tony made a mental note to ask Brody about it later. "Worry about getting Cody better, sir. The rest will work out on its own."

He tried to believe that. He had a feeling Cody would never ride bulls again. Tony hoped Cody would be able to reconcile the fact and learn to live a different life from the one he'd imagined.

Brody shook Mr Harwood's hand before they left the hospital. Tony tossed the keys to Brody as they got to the rental car.

"You can drive to the airport. I don't feel like it." He slid into the passenger seat and closed his eyes.

Brody started the car, pulled out of the parking lot and headed towards the airport. Tony didn't say anything for a few minutes. Brody's hand rested on his thigh, keeping him grounded. He entwined their fingers and sighed.

"Cody's fucked up, babe."

"I know." Brody's voice held sympathy.

"How is he going to be able to do anything?" Opening his eyes, he looked out of his window.

"You'd be surprised. Cody's going to get the best surgeons, therapists and equipment to help with his recovery and someday, he just might be riding again." Brody squeezed his hands. "Have a little faith, Tony."

"Faith?" He glanced at Brody. "How come all of Cody's hospital bills are taken care of?"

Brody shrugged. "I have money and so does Les. We're willing to help out those who don't have enough."

"Generous of you. What's the real reason?" He raised an eyebrow at Brody.

"I'll be honest. Watching Cody get thrown around like a ragdoll the other day scared me. I like you, Tony. I could find myself falling hard for you. I have to deal with the way Cody's injuries made me feel." Brody swallowed, staring straight ahead. "I don't know what I'd do if something like that happened to you. I have to make sure I can handle it."

"I get that, but it doesn't explain why you're paying Cody's hospital bills."

Tony was stubborn. His mother had often told him he could out-stubborn a mule. He wasn't going to let Brody off the hook.

"What if it had been you? Would you have the money to pay the bills?"

Tony shook his head. "No."

The truth was that for most bull riders and rodeo participants, health insurance was too high or they couldn't get insured at all because of the high risk of their profession. Only the top riders made any kind of money to help defray costs.

"Les and I talked the night of Cody's wreck. If it had been you, I'd hope someone would be willing to step in and help you. We decided to set up a fund to help with the costs of hospital bills or just competing. We might end up sponsoring a new rider."

"A new rider?" Tony pouted. "What about me?"

They stopped at a light and Brody glanced at him. Lifting their hands, Brody pressed a kiss to Tony's knuckles. "I'd love to put my name on you somewhere."

He laughed. "I'm sure you would, but I'm not looking to get branded."

"The reason we thought about sponsoring a new rider is because they're going to have a harder time finding endorsements and opportunities like those. You don't have that problem anymore."

The light turned green and Brody took off. Tony saw the logic in what Les and Brody were considering.

"You heading back to L.A. now?"

He ignored the loneliness he was already feeling. There was no way he or Brody could spend all their time with each other. They had lives elsewhere and he couldn't ask Brody to give up his life when he wasn't ready to change his own quite yet.

"Yes. I have two meetings this week." Brody pulled up in front of the terminal. "Where you headed this weekend?"

"Baltimore." He grabbed his bags out of the boot and handed them to the skycap. "Gonna rest up and I'll fly out on Thursday."

Brody nodded. "My gate's on the other side of the terminal."

Tony gave Brody a quick hug. He longed to be able to kiss his lover goodbye, but knew it wouldn't be well accepted by the people around them. "Give me a call later on tonight."

"I will. Have a safe trip home, Tony. Tell everyone I said hi." Brody ghosted his fingers over Tony's lips before he walked away.

Tony watched Brody drive off to return the car before he went to check in at the airline.

* * * *

Tony settled in the chair on the porch. He zipped up his coat and tugged out his pack of cigarettes. After lighting one, he took a drag and leant back. He rested his head on the chair, closing his eyes.

The door squeaked as someone came onto the porch. He didn't look. A hand touched his knee and he smiled.

"How's it going, Randy?"

"Good."

Opening his eyes, he looked at the man sitting at his feet. Randy leaned up against his legs. "Your lover send you out here to check on me?"

"No. I thought I'd come out and keep you company." Randy's blue eyes held a hint of concern for him.

"It's one of the fucking coldest nights of the winter and you decide to come out to keep me company." Tony laughed and shook his head. "I'm okay."

"Maybe." Randy didn't sound confident. "Did you talk to Cody's parents?"

"Right after dinner." He raised his gaze to the distant outline of the Rocky Mountains.

"Any news?" his friend asked cautiously.

"Yes, but it's not good." Tony scrubbed his hand over his face. "The swelling's gone down some and the doctors are pretty sure Cody broke his neck. The CAT scan they took earlier today showed what looks like a fracture. The doctors still don't know for sure how bad it is. I told his parents Cody squeezed my hand when I talked to him. That's a good sign, don't you think?"

Randy shrugged. "I would think so."

Tony shook his head. "Mr Harwood said it didn't mean anything except Cody's arms aren't paralysed."

"It is a good sign." Randy was trying to be encouraging. "At least he can move his hands."

"Doesn't mean he'll walk or ride again." Tony nodded over to where David Preston was walking to his truck. "Look at your friend, David."

"I know." Randy waved as his former travelling partner drove off. "David might not be able to compete anymore but at least he can walk and ride."

Tony sighed. "I know. It's hard to accept Cody won't be travelling with me anymore. Or I might not see him at an event again."

"It'll take time to get used to, but we both know things like this can happen every time you get on a bull or I got on a horse." Randy rested his hand on Tony's knee. "The risk of serious injury is one of the reasons we do what we do."

"I wish Brody hadn't been there to see the wreck." He took another puff on his smoke.

"Scared him?"

"A little. He said he wanted to think about this whole thing." He grinned down at Randy. "Brody's a city boy. He doesn't understand the point to bull riding, though he does appreciate the fact the boys wear tight jeans and chaps."

"Makes for nice scenery." Randy laughed with him.

His cell phone rang. After pulling it out of his pocket, he checked the number and saw it was Brody.

"Speak of the devil." He shook the phone a little.

"I'll leave you alone. Don't stay out too long. It's nasty cold out here."

He nodded and answered the phone. "Hey there, Blondie."

"Blondie, huh? Are you still paying me back for the sweet cheeks remark?" Brody chuckled.

"Maybe. How was your flight back home?" He crushed out his cigarette and tucked his free hand in his coat pocket.

"Boring." Brody sounded tired.

"Mine too." He stretched out, crossing his legs at the ankle and relaxed.

"Morgan and Vance were waiting for me at the airport. I ended up going in to the office and working until an hour ago."

What sounded like a door shutting came over the phone.

Tony set the chair rocking under him. "Business good?"

"There are days I think I was insane to start up my own business. I don't have a head for numbers and organisation." A soft grunt filled his ear.

Tony shivered and realised he'd been sitting outside for a while. Pushing to his feet, he moved inside. He stopped in the mud room to tug off his boots and hang up his jacket. "Did you want to talk to Yancey? I don't think he's gone to bed yet."

"No. I talked to him earlier. I called to talk to you." Brody's voice lowered.

His cheeks warmed and he knew it wasn't from the heat in the house. "Thanks for saying that."

"It's the truth." Brody yawned.

"You're worn out, big guy. Why don't you go to bed and I'll call you tomorrow?" Tony leaned against the kitchen counter and reached for a glass.

"I can barely keep my eyes open." Brody sighed. "I miss you already and it hasn't even been a day."

"In two weeks, I'm going to be in Tacoma, Washington. Maybe you could come and meet me up there for the weekend?"

He bit his lip. He hadn't wanted to sound pushy. Brody had made it clear he needed to think about the risks involved in what Tony did for a living and Tony respected his reservations. He'd seen the reality of competing destroy marriages and families. He didn't know yet if he and Brody would have that kind of relationship, but he wanted Brody to be sure about it before they went any further.

"Give me the dates tomorrow and I'll see about rearranging my schedule." Brody didn't seem upset with Tony for asking.

"Thanks." Tony turned to stare out of the window. "I know you wanted to think about the whole thing after Cody's wreck."

"I had plenty of time to do so on the flight home. I'll deal with being scared when you ride. It's something I'll have to get used to because I want to keep seeing you," Brody admitted.

A tightness Tony hadn't even known had been in his chest eased. "I'm glad to hear that."

He saw Les' reflection in the window as he entered the kitchen and headed for the refrigerator.

"Have a good night, Brody. I'll talk to you tomorrow."

"Night, Tony." Brody hung up.

Tony flipped his phone closed and slipped it into his back pocket. Les held out a beer to him. He shook his head.

"I think I'm going to bed."

"It's been a long weekend for you." Les hugged him before he left the kitchen. "We'll catch you tomorrow."

"Night."

He wandered down to his room, wondering if living in L.A. was a choice he'd consider.

Chapter Fourteen

Tacoma Classic, Tacoma, Washington

Brody threw his bag down on one of the hotel beds and flopped beside it. "Don't you get tired of travelling to a different town every week?"

Tony eased into the single chair in the room. "I do get tired, but this is my job. I don't go to an event, I don't get paid." He stared down at his boots.

After climbing to his feet, Brody walked over to kneel before him. "Let me help you get these off."

He grasped the back and the toe of Tony's boot, tugging. It slid off and he set it aside. After taking Tony's other boot off, Brody settled back on his heels.

"Why don't you get those clothes off? I'll start a bath for you." He squeezed Tony's knee. "I know you've got a couple of bruises and you should soak to relax those muscles."

"Good idea," Tony agreed.

After he stood, he brushed a kiss over the bull rider's lips. "You want some company?"

Tony cradled the back of Brody's head, urging him closer for another kiss. "I always want your company."

"Strip," Brody ordered, moving towards the bathroom.

The water was steaming as it filled the tub. He unbuttoned his shirt before tossing it through the open doorway towards the second bed. His jeans and underwear were next. Tony came in and Brody shut off the water.

"Climb in." He gestured to the tub. "Soak for a few minutes. I'll order us some room service."

"Thanks." Tony rested his head against the edge of the tub and closed his eyes.

Brody tried not to stare at the bruises marring Tony's olive skin. The bull his lover had ridden the night before in Portland had caught Tony in the chest with a glancing blow. The vest had saved Tony from a more serious injury.

He ordered food then went back into the bathroom. "The food will be up in a bit. Slide forward."

Tony sat up and moved, leaving room for Brody to slip in behind him. Brody's legs pressed against Tony's and he wrapped his arms around Tony's waist, letting his cowboy lean on him.

Rubbing his fingers over Tony's stomach, he nuzzled into the dark damp curls at the nape of Tony's neck, investigating the ridges outlining the muscles in Tony's abdomen.

"Sorry you didn't ride last night," he said softly.

Tony shrugged. "It happens. There's no way I can ride every bull. No rider is that good. I've been lucky this year and ridden more of them than bucked me off." Tony rested his head back on Brody's shoulder, giving Brody more skin to play with.

He nibbled along Tony's neck, tasting the sweat and water beading up on Tony's skin. Brody pulled away to ask, "What would be considered a good riding percentage?"

"Do you really feel like talking?" Tony's question was laced with laughter.

"At the moment, yes. You don't need me to fuck you right now. Relax. We'll get to the sex later." He reached down and squeezed Tony's balls gently.

"Hm-m-m..." Tony purred, rubbing his ass against Brody's cock.

"Easy, baby." Brody laid his hand in the middle of Tony's chest. "What would be a good percentage?"

"Fine." Tony pouted for a moment. "An awesome year would be riding sixty per cent, or close to it. More realistic is forty to fifty per cent. If I can ride half of the bulls I get on, I'll have a shot at the World Championship buckle at the end of the year."

"How long have you been riding bulls?" Brody grabbed a washcloth and soap, lathering it up.

"I've always wanted to do it, but I didn't actually start riding until I was eighteen. I've only been in the PBR for two years. Finished fifth at the finals last year. I'm doing better this year. I have to hope I don't get seriously injured and have to sit out for any length of time."

"Do you ever take time off to rest and heal up the bruises?" He ran the cloth over Tony's arm, down around each of the man's fingers.

"Sure. I might not go to Australia this year. I went last year and it was great, but the travel isn't much fun." Tony's body went limp as all the tension left.

"Let me know when you're taking the time, I'll arrange my schedule to fit in with yours."

Silence filled the air as Brody scrubbed Tony's chest. A knock sounded on the door. Brody pushed out of the tub and threw a robe on.

"I'll take care of this. Just take your time." Brody kissed the top of Tony's head and left.

Tony rinsed off and lifted the plug on the tub to let the water out. He stood, dried off and wrapped the towel around his waist. Wandering out of the bathroom, he smiled. Brody was setting plates out on the small hotel desk.

"I ordered us steak and potatoes. I figured you'd be hungry."

He trailed a hand over Brody's ass as he went to sit down at the desk. Brody had moved it from the wall so one of them could sit on the bed and the other could use the chair.

"Thanks." He sat on the bed.

"No problem. Here's a beer." Brody handed him a bottle.

After he took a swig, he set the bottle down then cut into the steak. He knew Brody had something to say to him by the way the blond kept looking at him. He finished his steak.

"Not the worst room service steak I've had," he commented as he settled back to the headboard. "What do you want to talk about?"

Brody looked surprised. "What do you mean?"

"You've been eyeing me since we checked in and I don't think it's just because you're lusting after my ass." Tony laughed at the blush colouring Brody's cheeks.

"Well, it is a nice ass." Brody pushed his steak all over his plate. "You're right. When we were in St

Louis, I talked to Les about finding a place for me in Wyoming."

"A place?" He frowned, not sure what Brody was talking about. "I'm sure Les and Randy wouldn't mind you staying at their place when you come to visit Yancey."

"Not a place at their ranch. A ranch of my own." Brody's gaze remained focused on the fork in his hand.

"You don't know anything about ranching. Why would you buy one?" He was really confused.

"Yancey wants to go to college in Wyoming." Brody sighed and set the fork down. His blue eyes were serious when they met Tony's gaze. "The truth is I thought you would like to stay in Wyoming close to Randy and Les."

Tony took a deep breath. "I would like to stay close to Randy and Les? Why does what I'd like affect where you live?"

Brody shot to his feet, pushing back from the table. Tony watched as he wandered over to the window. Brody turned, leaned against the windowsill and looked at him.

"I know we've only known each for a short amount of time and you can tell me I'm crazy, but I don't like sleeping alone anymore."

He shook his head. "You're not buying a ranch simply because you're tired of sleeping alone?"

"You're right. I'm tired of living in L.A.—I never planned on staying there forever. I can do my part of the business anywhere. I want to be around for Yancey. I know he's an adult and can take care of himself, but still, I want to hang out with him and get to know him." Brody came and sat down on the bed next to Tony. "If I'm living in Wyoming, we can see each other more often. I know Les doesn't mind us staying at their ranch, but I don't want to take advantage of his generous nature."

"I understand that." He wondered if he was hearing what he wanted in Brody's words.

"I thought you and Juan could move in with us." Brody took his hand.

"Um-m-m..." Tony didn't know what to say.

Brody chuckled. "I'm not asking you to marry me. You don't have to make a decision right away, either. I just wanted you to know what Les was doing for me and that the possibility is out there for you."

He squeezed Brody's hand. "Thanks. It's nice to know I have a place to go if I need one."

"We both know Randy and Les would let you live with them. They consider you a member of their family." Brody snuggled close to him, wrapping an arm around his waist.

"Yeah, they're good people. Maybe we shouldn't mention anything to Juan until we know for sure, because I don't want him to get his hopes up in case it doesn't happen." Tony tugged on Brody's robe. "Get this off and let's get to bed. I don't have to be at the arena until later on in the day. Are you planning on staying tomorrow night as well?"

Brody sat, untied the belt and slipped the robe off. Tony pulled the towel from around his waist and dropped it over the side of the bed. They climbed under the blankets. Once they were spooning together, Tony's back to Brody's chest, Brody answered him.

"Sure. I know the final round goes late, so I don't have a flight back to L.A. until Monday," Brody murmured, his lips moving against Tony's neck.

"Good." His eyes drifted shut.

"This is what I miss most."

Tony smiled at the softly spoken words. He understood how Brody felt.

* * * *

Something dropped on Tony's face. He frowned, reaching up to wipe it off. A set of hands grabbed his and pushed them back onto the bed.

"No moving except for your hips."

He became completely awake at Brody's words. Brody braced his body over him, buried in his ass. Another drop of sweat hit Tony's face. Tony relished the feeling of fullness, but it was quite surprising that Brody could stretch him and press into him without him waking up before this. He arched his hips, encouraging Brody to ride him.

Lifting his legs, he wrapped them around Brody's waist, digging his heels into Brody's ass cheeks. "Harder."

"With pleasure."

Brody slid his hands under Tony's ass, angling them so each thrust in nailed Tony's gland. Tony flexed his muscles, creating the right kind of friction for his lover.

"Right there." He grunted, his eyes rolling back in his head.

Their movements synced and he bore down while Brody pushed in. The room filled with the sound of skin slapping skin. Scents of sweat and sex perfumed the air. He knew he would come without touching his own cock. Brody bent and licked his nipple, before biting it hard enough for pain to course through him and heighten his pleasure.

"Fuck."

Brody shot him a wicked wink and went to tease Tony's other nipple. Tony gripped the blankets under him. Lightning shot through his body, tracing through every nerve ending to pool at the base of his spine. The pressure built and drew his balls tight to his body.

"Please." He opened his eyes to see a grimace on Brody's face and knew Brody's own release would be soon. "I want us to come together."

"I'll be with you when you do." Brody's teeth were clenched.

He leaned up, crushing their lips together. Tony came. His cum spilled from his dick, coating his stomach and chest. Brody slammed into him and climaxed.

When Tony finished wringing the last bit of Brody's pleasure from him, he fell onto the bed. Brody followed him, managing to brace his body by placing his hands on either side of Tony's head. Panting, they stared at each other. Sweat dripped from Brody's face to mingle with Tony's.

"We should get tested." He bit his lip.

Fuck, sex seemed to have switched off his 'thinking before he spoke' button.

"Good idea. I'd like to feel you fuck me without rubber getting in the way." Brody gave him a short kiss.

"I've never done it without protection." He unhooked his ankles and dropped his legs down with a sigh.

"Neither have I. I've never found any guy I'd been willing to risk it for."

Brody pulled away from him and left the bed to take care of the condom. Tony looked up at the dark ceiling and thought about what he'd suggested. To fuck without protection was a huge step. It spoke of trust and a depth of caring he never thought he'd achieve with any man.

If he was willing to get tested and start having sex without a condom, then what was stopping him from moving in with Brody when the man found a ranch to buy in Wyoming? Tony realised the choice of Wyoming truly was because of him. Brody could have found property back in Austin or somewhere else, but he'd chosen Wyoming so Tony wouldn't miss his friends.

"You're thinking too hard." Brody tossed a wet washcloth to him.

He caught it, cleaned up then threw it back to Brody who took it back into the bathroom. Brody glanced out at him.

"I'm taking a shower. I want to head out and grab some breakfast."

He waited until the water started before he climbed out of bed and tugged on his jeans. He pulled out his phone and his cigarettes. Finding paper and a pen, he left Brody a note saying he was having a cigarette outside.

Lighting his cigarette, he leaned against the building and hit speed dial.

"Hey, Tony," Randy answered.

"How ya' doing, cowboy?" He dragged in a breath of smoke.

"Good. Folsom dumped my ass three times in the arena. I almost got trampled by the herd of steers. Other than that, I'm fine. We'll see what else happens during the rest of the day."

Tony let the back of his head bump the brick wall behind him. "Sounds kind of rough. You letting Les take care of you?"

Home of His Own

Randy laughed. "Of course. I'm going to convince him to kiss my bruises later."

"I don't think you'll have to work too hard on convincing him." Tony drew in some smoke and blew it out. "Brody's looking for a ranch in Wyoming close to you."

"I know. Les told me," Randy admitted.

"You knew? Why didn't you say something?" He couldn't believe Randy hadn't mentioned it to him.

"It's none of my business, Tony."

Randy's voice faded away and Tony could barely hear him talking to someone.

"Didn't you think I'd want to know?"

"No. As much as Brody's doing this for you, he's doing it for Yancey as well," Randy pointed out.

"True. He asked me to move in with him."

"Wow. Next thing you know, you'll be getting married."

Randy's teasing made him smile.

"Shut up, asshole." He ground his cigarette out on the sidewalk. "I shouldn't over-think this, should I?"

"You're right. I think you and Brody are building something solid, but if it doesn't work out, you always have a place with Les and me." Randy groaned.

"I know." He pulled open the door. "I'll let you go. Take care of those bruises and tell Les hi for me. Let Juan know I'll call him after the go-around."

"Will do. Have a good ride today." Randy hung up.

He slid the card in the lock and made his way into the hotel room. Brody was lying on the bed, ankles crossed, watching TV. His lover grinned at him.

"How are Randy and Les doing?"

He stripped his jeans off before padding towards the bathroom. "They're good. I'll grab a quick shower and we can get breakfast afterwards."

Brody nodded and winked as Tony shut the bathroom door.

Chapter Fifteen

Brody settled into his seat at the arena. He'd dropped Tony off at the rider's entrance and parked the rental. He opened his programme and studied the riders. While they'd been having breakfast, Tony had told him about the other riders and who would present the biggest challenge to his winning the World Championship buckle.

"I see you're here."

He looked up to see the lady from the St Louis event standing next to him. Brody stood and held out his hand.

"Good to see you again, ma'am."

She laughed. "I'm Sally Howard. I see we're sitting next to each other again as well." Sally shook his hand and sat down.

"Brody MacCafferty. I didn't see you last night." He took his seat and leant forward, resting his elbows on his knees. He glanced down into the arena at the bucking chutes, trying to spot Tony.

"Had some other business to take care of." Sally opened her programme and circled some of the pictures. "You don't strike me as a rodeo fan, even though I hear a hint of Texas in your voice." Sally pulled a camera out of her bag along with a notebook and pen.

"I'm not. Just started watching the PBR this year. I met Tony last year in Hawaii." Brody didn't know how much to say. He knew there was no way he could explain that Tony had picked him up at a bar. "Ended up running into each other in St Louis. I do business all over the country."

"Do you think I could get him to give me an interview?"

He swore silently. Damn his luck. He had to befriend a reporter. "I don't know. You'd have to ask him."

"I'll try and track him down. I cover the PBR for my home town newspaper in Kansas." Sally grinned and winked at him. "Can't beat it. They pay me to wander around the country, asking handsome cowboys about riding bulls."

"Not a bad job if you can get it, I guess." He knew he had to watch what he said—there was no point in getting a reporter digging around Tony.

"Well, maybe not for you, but for me, it's a dream come true." She checked her watch. "The round should be starting soon."

He stayed silent.

"Hey, Romanos is friends with Cody Harwood, right? How's the kid doing?"

Brody wasn't sure how much he should say. "As good as could be expected. I'm sure if you talked to someone from the association, they could tell you more."

"Maybe. I'll find someone." Sally eased forward in her seat as the first bull was run into the chute.

He relaxed slightly. With the round starting, she shouldn't be interested in talking to him. He could concentrate on Tony and watching all that prime male flesh wander around the arena. All of the cowboys who came to the events were wonderful eye candy.

Ten riders in, it was Tony's turn. Brody checked the bull's name. Chicken Little. He chuckled. "Where do they come up with some of these names?"

Sally turned to wink. "The contractors get a little desperate when they breed so many. Of course, it's really only the ones who become classic bulls or big-time bulls who get named."

"I didn't know it was such a big business." He watched Tony pull his rope tight around Chicken Little's red stomach.

"When it all started, there wasn't money to be made doing this, or breeding bulls for that matter. Now a bull as good or as rank as Tank's Reward could sell for hundreds of thousands of dollars. Not to mention stud fees."

He nodded towards the medium-sized bull Tony was getting a seat on. "What about Chicken Little?"

"He's a money bull."

"A money bull?" He needed to buy a notebook and start writing down these terms.

"Yep. The cowboys tend to win money when they ride him. He's ridden a lot, but you can get high marks off him. There are four judges who award a hundred points. Fifty for the rider and fifty for the bull. You want a bull that bucks hard and spins well. You also would like him to do some direction changes. Mix things up a little." Sally gestured to Tony. "I'd bet on Romanos riding this bull every time."

Brody hoped it wasn't bad luck. He gripped the back of the seat in front of him as Tony pushed down his hat and nodded to the gate man. The red bull leapt out of the gate and Tony rode the spin to the left perfectly. One huge jump rode Tony back off his bull rope.

"He's losing the rope," Sally pointed out.

"What does that mean?" Brody didn't take his eyes off Tony.

"His grip is slipping."

He nodded and air caught in his lungs as Tony's hand popped out of the bull rope. His lover went flying over the bull's head and ploughed face first into the dirt. The bullfighters came running in, sacrificing their own bodies to distract the bull from Tony. Brody watched Tony jump to his feet and stagger to the fence. Brody bit back a groan when he saw blood drip off the end of Tony's nose.

"I think he might have hurt his shoulder."

He glanced at Sally with a frown. "What makes you think that?"

"Look at the way he's holding his left arm close to his body." She nodded down towards Tony.

Brody looked back at his bull rider. Tony cradled his left arm with his right and let the medical guys help him out of the arena. When Tony disappeared behind the chutes, Brody sat back and scrubbed his face with his hand.

He'd seen cowboys get hung up in their bull ropes. They'd been stomped on, tossed around like a salad and body slammed into the dirt. He still remembered how worried he'd been when Cody had nearly been killed by Tank's Reward.

None of those emotions could top how he felt at the moment when he'd watched his lover helped out of the arena with blood pouring down his face.

"What should I do?" he asked, unsure what to do or where to go.

"Wait. Someone will come and get you. Especially if they send Romanos to the hospital for X-rays." Sally reached out and patted his shoulder. "It'll be okay."

"Are you Brody MacCafferty?" A voice broke through Brody's stunned focus.

For the first time in his life, he wished he was a woman. Then he could freak out without anyone looking at him funny.

"Brody, breathe." Sally jabbed her elbow in his side.

He sucked in a deep breath and nodded at the older cowboy.

"Yeah."

"They want to transport Romanos to the hospital. He wants to see you before he leaves and I'll get you directions."

Brody nodded with a shaky smile. "It's not serious, is it?"

The PBR official shook his head and turned, leading the way out of the arena seats and behind the bucking chutes. "Nah, it's just precautionary. He has a separated shoulder and a cut over his eye. Shoulder will force him out for a month or so. Though I doubt he'll take that long."

Brody vowed to do whatever it took to keep Tony off the tour until his shoulder was fully healed. They arrived at the medical room on time to hear Tony complain.

"I don't need to get X-rays, Doc. I'm fine. Nothing else is broken or dislocated. My shoulder's killing me though."

Brody walked in and his mouth dropped open. Tony stood bare-chested, glaring up at the head doctor. Brody let his gaze trace over the rest of Tony's body, noting new bruises and scratches, plus the way his lover held his left arm tight to his body.

"We don't know for sure if your shoulder's dislocated or if it's broken. That's why you need to get X-rays. We could do more damage if we put it back in now." The doctor didn't back down.

Tony's chin tilted at a familiar stubborn angle and Brody knew he had to step in.

"Go to the hospital, Romanos. This event is fucked for you anyway. It won't hurt and could save problems later." Brody gave Tony's uninjured shoulder a quick squeeze.

"Doc, this is Brody MacCafferty," Tony introduced them. The cowboy grimaced when he tried to move his arm. "This fucking hurts."

"I know." At Tony's sceptical look, he laughed. "I'm a bodyguard, Tony. I've been injured as many times as you. So just go to the hospital."

"Wow. You've hit the big time if you need a bodyguard around." The doctor chuckled.

"He's a friend, Doc." Tony met Brody's gaze.

Brody hoped his cowboy could see all the love and concern he felt for him.

Tony sighed. "Fine. I'll go to the hospital, but Brody will drive me there. Call to let them know I'm coming." Tony grabbed his torn shirt off a table.

"Thanks for convincing the stubborn bastard to go." The doctor slapped Brody on the shoulder as he went by.

"Tony's not stupid, just pig-headed." Brody winked at his lover.

"Smartass," Tony grumbled.

As they collected the directions to the hospital, Brody noticed Tony's olive skin growing paler the longer it took them to leave. He placed his hand at the small of Tony's back for a second. Leaning down, he whispered, "A few more minutes, love."

Tony nodded, but kept silent. Brody wanted to wrap his arm around Tony's waist and support him. He figured the other cowboys might frown on that, unless Tony had a leg injury.

They got settled in the truck. He pulled out his cell phone and handed it to Tony. "Call Randy and Les—let them know what happened."

Brody climbed behind the wheel and put the key in. Tony shook his head and set the phone beside him.

"No. You can call them while I'm getting X-rayed."

Brody left the parking lot. Reaching over, he rested his hand on Tony's thigh. "It's been hard not touching you this time," he admitted, squeezing the firm muscle.

"Trust me, I understand. All I wanted to do when I saw you standing there was to throw myself at you and let you hold me." Tony covered Brody's hand with his good one.

"You're okay." He laughed at Tony's sceptical look. "Well, except for the shoulder. Nothing broken, not like Cody."

"Thank God it wasn't Tank's Reward I was on. That SOB would've stomped my ass into the ground." Tony leant back and grimaced. "I want painkillers and a shower. I've got dirt in places dirt shouldn't be."

He leered at Tony. "I'll help take care of that problem when we get back to the hotel."

"I'll take you up on that." Tony closed his eyes.

"Try to relax. The doctor said the hospital wasn't too far from the arena."

Brody let silence fill the cab as they sped along. He wanted Tony to rest and not try to talk. Every once in a while Tony's grip would tighten on his fingers. He'd had a few dislocated shoulders in his bouncer's career, so he understood how Tony was feeling.

He saw the hospital lights. "Tony, we're here."

Tony sat up with a grimace. "Pull up outside the entrance. I'll start the paperwork while you park the truck."

"Sure."

Brody stopped outside the doors and watched Tony climb out of the truck. He thought about offering to help, but decided against it. His lover could take care of himself and if Brody put his arm around Tony, he wasn't sure he'd let the man go.

Tony nodded at him before opening the glass door. Brody found the closest parking spot, locked the truck then headed inside. Tony was getting the paperwork from the nurse to fill out when Brody got to the desk.

"Shit. This is turning out to be an expensive year." Tony sighed, trying to hold the clipboard on his lap while writing without moving his left arm.

"Here." Brody reached for his wallet and pulled out his insurance card.

"You're not paying for me." Tony didn't glance at the card.

"I'm not paying for you. I'm helping you out," Brody said.

The clipboard slid to the floor with a clang. Tony tried to catch it and Brody watched as Tony's cheeks went pale.

"Fuck."

Brody shook his head. "Don't move. Let me get it."

Tony closed his eyes and clenched his teeth. Brody didn't care who might see them. He placed his hand on Tony's knee and squeezed. He waited until Tony looked at him before he spoke.

"Where's your wallet?"

"In my bag out in the truck."

He nodded. Made sense. Tony wasn't going to ride a bull with a wallet in his pocket.

"I'll run out and grab it for you." He handed Tony the forms. "Take your time and if you hurt, stop. I can finish filling it out when I get back in."

Brody walked out to the truck.

"Stubborn-ass cowboy," he muttered, digging through Tony's equipment bag for the man's wallet. He grabbed it from under Tony's glove.

He zipped the bag closed, slammed the truck door closed then turned. Tony stood behind him.

"What the hell were you thinking? I would have come and helped you."

Tony waved a hand in the direction of an orderly going into the hospital. Brody slid his arms around Tony's waist and let the man lean on him. He ran his hands up and down Tony's back, wishing he could have Tony naked, pressed against him. Brody knew touch offered more comfort than words.

Brushing a kiss over Tony's temple, he hugged him tight for a second and stepped away. "Let's get you in there. We'll have the doctor check you out and then I'm taking you to the hotel."

"I'm sorry." Tony didn't fight him as he led the bull rider inside.

"Why?" He lifted the clipboard from Tony's seat and gestured for him to sit down.

"I know you're trying to help." Tony nodded towards the forms. "I'm not used to anyone being around to take care of me. Les and Randy would, but they don't travel with me very often."

"You've taken care of yourself for most of your life and I respect that, but you have to know when to let someone else do for you. I'm not giving you charity or pity." Brody cupped Tony's face with his hand. "I care about you, Tony, and when you're hurt, I want to help out."

Tony nuzzled into Brody's hand for a second before he finished filling out the forms. Tony was called back only a few minutes after turning the clipboard in. The nurse wanted to take him up to X-ray right away.

Brody dug out his phone. "I'll call the guys and let them know what's going on."

"Thanks. I'll have them come and get you when I'm in the room." Tony smiled at him.

He wandered outside to lean against the building and dialled the ranch.

"Hardin Ranch," Margie answered.

"Hey, Margie. It's Brody. Is Juan around anywhere?"

"Hello, Mr MacCafferty. I believe he's in his room doing homework. I'll go get him."

"Thanks." He rested his head on the brick of the hospital and closed his eyes.

It was a few minutes before he heard the phone get picked up again.

"Brody?"

"Hey, Juan. How's school going?" Brody rubbed his eyes hard.

"Good. Why are you calling me and not *Tío* Tony?" Fear tainted Juan's question.

"He's in getting X-rays." The silence on the other end of the phone made him rush to assure Juan. "Don't worry, kid. He has a dislocated shoulder, but they're just making sure it's not broken. He'll probably need some stitches as well."

"It's been a rough start to the season for him, hasn't it?" Juan sounded relieved.

"Yeah. I hope things get better soon. I'm not sure I can take him being injured again," Brody admitted.

"You know, I've talked to Dusty and Burt. It sounds like he'll have a ton of injuries, but mostly minor ones. Pulled muscles, sprains and things like that."

"That's good to know. Can you give the rest the news? I'll have Tony call you when we get back to the hotel."

"Sure. Thanks, Brody. I'm glad you're there with him." Juan hung up.

Brody slipped his phone in his pocket and went inside to wait for the nurse to call him back.

* * * *

"Tony, stop." Brody laughed, trying to push the bull rider away from him.

"Why?" Tony's dark eyes sparkled as the man licked Brody's cock from base to tip.

"You're injured. We spent three hours in the hospital getting you X-rayed and your shoulder popped back in place. Do you really want to ruin all that hard work?" Brody made sure not to hit Tony's shoulder as he urged Tony to lie on the bed.

"No, but I want you." Tony pouted.

Brody ran his finger over Tony's bottom lip. "Well, when you put it that way, go ahead. Knock yourself out."

Tony's face lit up and he started to slide down the bed.

"Wait."

"What now?" Tony frowned at him.

"I was kidding about going ahead." Brody stopped the words from pouring out of Tony's mouth by placing a finger over his lips. "Do you want me to fuck you?"

Tony nodded.

"I think you need to ride me. Best way to do it so you're not putting any pressure on that shoulder." He ran his fingers over the bruise discolouring Tony's skin.

"Works for me." Tony reached for the lube sitting on the nightstand.

The lube landed on Brody's chest. Brody was happy they had managed to get tested when they had had some time in between jobs and events. He shook his head when Tony straddled his hips.

"You're a bit of a slut, aren't you?"

"Are you complaining?"

Popping the top off the lube, Brody laughed. He squirted some on his fingers and rubbed them together. "No. We're a perfect match since I like fucking you as much as you seem to like being fucked."

Tony hummed as Brody pressed one finger against his ass. Inch by inch, he worked the digit further into Tony's passage. Tony braced a hand on his chest and rocked, relaxing with each backward push.

"H-m-m-m...doesn't matter. As long as there's coming involved, I don't care how we get there."

Brody chuckled. "That's true."

He slid two fingers in, stretching Tony's hole and spreading the lube into the tight channel. Tony stared down at him, biting his bottom lip as they worked together to get Tony ready for Brody's cock.

"Now, Brody." Tony's cheeks flushed.

Tony rested his right hand on Brody's chest, easing down while Brody held his shaft. His lover didn't stop until he was in Tony. They sighed.

Tony clenched and Brody felt his breathing stop for a moment.

"Move."

He wasn't going to disobey the order. He gripped Tony's hips and lifted the man up until just the head of his cock rested inside the ring of muscle. Arching his hips, he drove back into Tony, nailing his lover's gland with the first stroke.

"Fuck." Tony's fingers flexed, his nails digging into Brody's skin.

Brody's mind short-circuited when Tony's muscles massaged his cock. He took Tony hard and fast, thanking God for Tony's balance and ability to ride bucking bulls or he would have knocked the guy off several times. He braced his feet against the mattress and pushed up, loving the feel of Tony's warmth sliding up and down on his shaft.

"Brody," Tony gasped his name.

He could tell his cowboy was ready to come. Tony's olive skin flushed red and he threw his head back, groaning as strings of cum shot from his cock. Brody kept moving, thrusting and drawing Tony's climax out. Or at least he tried to, but Tony's muscles' almost painful grip on his own dick drove all thought out of his mind and he came with a shout of his own.

Waiting until his brain straightened itself out, Brody ran his hands over Tony's hips and back. Tony eased down on him, their stomachs and chests sealed together with cum and sweat. Once their breathing had evened out, he rolled Tony over and slid out, carefully trying to not jostle Tony and his injured shoulder. Tony whimpered slightly.

"Hush, love. Let me clean us up and you can go to sleep."

He washed them both off. By the time he got back in bed, Tony was sound asleep. Brody brushed a kiss over Tony's injured shoulder and curled up beside him. He drifted to sleep as well, exhausted from worry and fear.

Chapter Sixteen

One week later, Hardin Ranch, Wyoming

Tony leaned against the porch railing, smoking and watching Yancey and Juan wander around the barns. He smiled when Yancey took Juan's hand.

Taking a deep breath, he caught Brody's spicy scent right before two arms wrapped around his waist and he was surrounded by warmth.

"I'm glad you could fly out," he admitted, relaxing back against his lover.

"So am I. I know Yancey could have looked at the ranches Les' real estate agent wanted to show us. I trust his judgement, and yours for that matter." Brody nuzzled Tony's ear. "But it gave me one more reason to come for a visit."

"You must be racking up the miles." He tilted his head, giving Brody more access to his skin.

"Don't mind. Not if it means I get to see you at the end."

Tony shivered. It turned him on to know Brody was so into him that Brody would travel hundreds of miles to see him.

A laugh drew his attention. He nodded to where Yancey and Juan were silhouetted by the afternoon sun. Brody chuckled. Yancey embraced Juan much like Brody was doing with Tony. Juan was pointing something out to Yancey.

"Do you remember what it was like being in love for the first time?" Brody's question was soft.

Tony shrugged. "It was the most agonising time of my life."

"Really?" Brody sounded surprised. "It was exhilarating for me. I'd finally found someone who was like me. I wasn't a freak. It was the best month of my teenage years."

Tony shifted, trying to move away. He didn't want to discuss the first boy he loved.

"I'm glad you had a good experience. Not everyone is so lucky." He tried to keep the bitterness out of his voice.

"What happened, Tony?" Brody sucked on the sensitive skin behind his ear.

"I don't want to talk about it. Let's just leave it with the fact that it scarred me for life and move on." He turned, wrapped his arms around Brody's neck and said, "Why don't we talk about the hot guy I'm in lust with now?"

The minute the words came out of his mouth, he felt the deceit in them. He didn't just lust after Brody. He loved the man and it scared him a little. As much as he'd made comments about finding the kind of love Randy and Les had, he had never believed he would. Who knew a one-night stand would end up being a man he could spend the rest of his life with?

Brody smiled at him. "I'll let it slide for now, but we will be talking about it again."

There were ways to keep Brody distracted enough for as long as it took for the man to forget about Tony's disastrous first love.

"Do you think they've had sex yet?" Brody nodded out towards the younger men.

Tony shook his head. "No. Yancey wouldn't do that. He'll wait."

"Why? They're young and think they're in love. Straight teenagers would be having sex every chance they got." Brody frowned.

"And we haven't done anything to make them think sex is bad, but Yancey is an adult. Juan isn't. It's as simple as that." Tony rested his hand on Brody's chest.

"Yancey's not an adult."

Brody's weak protest made Tony chuckle.

"He's eighteen, Brody, plus he's done more illegal things than you and I combined. Your brother isn't going to risk anything by rushing into sex." Tony shook his head. "Besides, as much as Juan might love him, my nephew isn't ready for anything that serious."

"How do you know that?" Brody asked.

Tony pushed on the wide chest in front of him, making Brody back up into the house. Les and Randy had disappeared into their bedroom shortly after lunch, so he wasn't worried about running into them.

"Trust me. I know."

He waited until they were inside the mud room before he wrapped one arm around Brody's neck and drew the man's mouth down to his. Tony's shoulder ached and he was glad he'd decided to take two weeks off. He would have to get back on tour soon, though. He couldn't let the other riders get a lead on him. The way Brody used his tongue drove any other thoughts out of his mind.

As Tony kissed Brody, he enjoyed the shivers racking Brody's body. He wormed his way under Brody's shirt and rested his hands against Brody's warm skin.

"Shit. Your hands are cold." Brody jerked.

Tony grinned and winked. "I know how to warm them up."

"Do you now? Don't you have something to do? Like ride a bull or something?"

He reached down and palmed Brody's erection through his jeans. "Oh, I know a bull I'd like to ride and it doesn't involve leaving the house."

"H-m-m-m…" Brody groaned and dragged him down the hallway towards their bedroom.

He grinned. There was no better way to spend a chilly afternoon than in the arms of a gorgeous man.

* * * *

Later that night

The doorbell rang as Tony started to cross the hall into the living room. "I'll get it," he yelled.

His mouth fell open when he saw his sister, Angelina, standing on the porch.

"Did you know?" Accusation and devastation warred in her eyes.

"Know what?" A sinking feeling in his stomach suggested he might have a clue.

"About Luis?" She glared at him, her hands clutching her purse.

He sighed and dropped his gaze for a moment. Tony didn't want to talk about it.

"You did know."

Her voice held defeat. Tony looked up to see tears running down her cheeks. He pushed the door open wider, gesturing for her to come inside.

"We aren't going to discuss this on the porch. I'll tell you everything you think you want to hear."

Angelina entered and handed him her coat and purse.

"Tony, who's at the door?"

Tony cringed when Brody came out into the hallway. Angelina gasped and Brody frowned at him.

"Brody, this is my older sister, Angelina Martinez. Angelina, this is my lover, Brody MacCafferty." He'd be damned if he denied who Brody was.

"It's nice to meet you, Mrs Martinez." Brody offered his hand while shooting a puzzled gaze at Tony.

Tony figured she would refuse to touch Brody, but he was shocked when she shook hands and offered his lover a hesitant smile.

"Nice meeting you."

"Brody, would you go and ask Margie if she'll make some tea and bring it to Les' study?"

"Sure. I'll let the others know." Brody gave him a quick smile before heading towards the kitchen.

Tony led Angelina to Les' study. He didn't want to talk about Luis in front of his friends. He'd just got her seated when Juan burst in with Yancey right behind him. Tony glared at the young men.

"Sorry, Tony. I told him to stay out of it." Yancey gave him an apologetic smile.

"I won't go back, *Tía* Angelina," Juan declared, his chin set at a defiant angle.

"As amazing as it might sound, *mijo*, Angelina isn't here to talk about you." Tony pointed to the door. "You can go now."

"Why are you here, then?" Juan frowned, resisting Yancey's attempts to get him out of the room.

"Luis." Angelina's eyes filled with tears again.

"Oh."

Tony was puzzled by the panicked look Juan shot Yancey. He made a mental note to ask what it was about later. He wanted to calm Angelina down first.

"Get him out of here," he ordered Yancey.

"Come on, Juan." Yancey nodded to Angelina and dragged Tony's nephew out of the study.

Margie delivered the tea, taking only enough time to pour a cup for Angelina. After the housekeeper left, the two siblings stared at each other. Finally, his sister broke the silence.

"Why didn't you tell me?"

The defeated tone of Angelina's voice hurt Tony. She'd never wavered in her beliefs, even if they might have been wrong, and to see her doubt herself now was hard to deal with. Anger flared. He wanted to go, find Luis and beat his ass.

"Would you have believed me?" He met his sister's gaze.

Angelina started to say something and he stopped her.

"Think before you say a word. You were the first to turn away when I came out. I found out about your wedding from *Tía* Elena. I wanted to rush home and tell you the truth when I heard it was Luis you were marrying, but I knew you wouldn't listen."

"What truth, Antonio? You mean you knew about Luis all those years ago?" Angelina looked shocked.

"Luis was the reason I told our parents when I was fifteen. He was my first everything. My first kiss, fuck, love and heartbreak. He was all of those." Tony stood and stalked to the window. Bracing his hands on the windowsill, he rested his forehead against the cool glass. "Your husband is the reason I lost my family and home."

"Ex-husband, or soon-to-be," Angelina murmured. "In all these years, you never thought to inform me about him?"

"When exactly would have been a good time? After the birth of your first child? Or when Papa went in for open heart surgery?" He turned to glare at her. "Please, tell me when would have been the perfect time for me to call you and say, 'By the way, Angelina, your husband cheats on you with other men. On those business trips he takes. All those nights he worked late in Austin, he was at some club, screwing around with some twink'."

The mention of clubs made Tony pause. Juan and Yancey had met in Austin at a club. Oh hell, he hoped Yancey had never met Luis.

"How could I tell you Luis didn't think of it as cheating because it was just some fag he fucked? Not another woman, so it didn't count." He went and knelt down in front of Angelina, gripping her hands. "How could I stand there and tell you when I was one of those fags?"

Her dark eyes, so much like his own, filled with sorrow. "I'm going to divorce him."

"I'm sorry." It was the only thing he could think of to say. "What did you tell Mama and Papa?"

"Just that Luis wasn't the man I thought he was."

He smiled grimly. "You're right. He's queer."

Shaking her head, Angelina squeezed his hands. "That's not what I meant. Luis might not think it's cheating because it's not a woman, but it is to me. I don't care if it was another woman, man or a dog, he broke his vows and I won't stay in a marriage like that."

"I hit him." Tony did nothing to hide the pride he felt at that accomplishment. "When he came here, asking me to come down."

"Luis said you came on to him and when he refused, you hit him." Angelina studied him. "Somehow, I doubt that's what happened."

"You're right. He kissed me and I pushed him away. I only hit him after he made some rude comments about you." Tony ducked his head and grinned. "I might have walked away from my family, but I'll be damned if anyone's going to talk shit about them."

Angelina lifted his chin and smiled. "Thank you, Antonio. We turned away as well. I'm sorry for that. Families should love each other, no matter what."

He took a chance and kissed her cheek. "I learnt that."

After climbing to his feet, he went to lean on Les' desk. "You're welcome to stay here. Did you rent a car at the airport?"

"No. I drove from Texas." Angelina picked up her cup then sipped the tea.

"Shit, Angelina! You drove all the way by yourself? What were you thinking?" Thoughts of what could have happened to her shot through his head.

"I had to see you. After I confronted Luis, I couldn't get rid of the belief you somehow knew about him and that was why you never showed up for our wedding." Angelina challenged him. "Was it?"

"It was one reason." He shrugged. "The other was I figured no one really wanted me there. *Tía* Elena has been the only close relative who has made me feel they care. I let go of any ties to you when I ran away."

Angelina looked sad.

He laughed. "Don't feel sad, Angelina. I wandered for eight years, looking for a place to lay my head. I wanted to find one place where I'd be welcomed with open arms and missed when I was gone." He gestured to the room around them. "I found it. Randy and Les made me a member of their family along with Brody, Yancey and Juan."

Tony went back to his sister and held out his hand. "I'd love to have my big sister back in my life. But," he warned, "you'll have to fit in with my family here. I won't allow you to hurt or upset them."

She took his peace offering, accepting his hand. "I understand. I'm not saying it'll be easy, but I'd like to start over." She hugged him.

He embraced her, his heart happy for the moment. "Good. Now, come on. I'm sure you're exhausted and by now, Margie's probably already got one of the guest rooms made up for you. I'll introduce you to the others tomorrow after you've rested."

Brody was standing on the other side of the door when Tony opened it, hand raised to knock. His lover looked at him with concern and he smiled, letting Brody know things were okay.

"Margie said to tell you the room's ready. Also, there's a nightgown and an extra toothbrush in the bathroom for you, Mrs Martinez," Brody told Angelina.

"Please, call me Angelina, and it'll be Romanos after the divorce is final." She touched Brody's arm. "I look forward to getting to know you better."

Brody's surprise showed on his face, but he nodded. "I'm sure we'll have time soon." Brody kissed Tony's cheek. "I'll be in the living room."

He watched Brody make his way back towards the front of the house. He caught Angelina watching them. He couldn't tell what she was thinking.

"Your room's down here." He led the way down the hall. "How did you find out about Luis?"

"*Tía* Elena can be a vindictive person when she feels someone has hurt her family." Angelina grimaced. "She asked me to drive her to Austin. Her directions managed to get us lost and we ended up outside a club. Luis was kissing some man in the crowd."

"That had to be a shock," he commented.

"I wanted to throw up. I couldn't believe he'd cheat on me. Where have I been all these years and how blind was I?" She shook her head. "*Tía* Elena never liked Luis. She told me my husband has hurt our family enough and deserves to be treated like the dog he is. I took her home and confronted him when he got home."

Tony opened the door to Lindsay's old room. "You can sleep here tonight."

"Thanks." Angelina stepped into the room then turned around. "When I accused him of cheating, Luis was furious. He yelled about that fag spilling his guts. He had to be talking about you. He was so angry, I got frightened and left. I called Mama and Papa to tell them I was getting a divorce. After I hung up on them, I called Elena and asked where you lived now."

"And she told you," Tony supplied the words.

"Yes. I drove straight here." A yawn interrupted her.

"Call Mama. Let her know you're okay. It's up to you whether you tell her where you are." He kissed her cheek. "Sleep as late as you want. We'll talk more tomorrow."

"Thank you, *mi hermano.* I don't deserve your kindness."

"Yes, you do. You're *mi hermana.* No matter what happened before."

He waited until she had shut her door before he headed back to the living room.

Brody stood when Tony came into the room. He watched as his lover went to the side bar, poured a double shot of whisky and slammed it back. Two more disappeared in similar fashion and Brody shot Les a worried look. Les shook his head.

Tony propped his body against the cabinet and took a deep breath. Brody moved over to stand next to him, resting his hand on a slumped shoulder.

"Are the boys still awake?" Tony's question was low, but Brody heard it.

"Yes. They went out to check on one of the mares. She's ready to drop her foal any time now." Brody rubbed his hand over Tony's shirt, trying to comfort his cowboy.

"Randy, call down to the barn and have them come in. We need to talk." Tony turned, wrapped his arms around Brody's waist and held tight.

Brody crushed Tony to his chest, not caring if all of the air in his lungs was being squeezed out. He held on, letting Tony know he was there for him.

"They're on their way in." Randy touched Brody's arm. "Les and I are going to bed."

"No." Tony pulled away. "We're family and there shouldn't be secrets among us."

Les took Randy's hand. "We'll go make some coffee."

Brody waited until the couple had left before he asked, "What the hell is going on, Tony?"

"I'll explain everything as soon as the boys get in here." Tony cupped his face. "I promise no one is dying or dead. But if I see my brother-in-law any time soon, that might be a lie."

"*Tío*?"

Juan and Yancey came in, worried frowns on their faces.

"Go wash up and come back. We need to talk," Tony said.

Yancey shot Brody a glance and he nodded. Whatever was going on was important to Tony and Brody would make sure it happened.

They all arrived back at the living room at the same time. Randy and Les had the coffee and mugs. The boys carried plates with pieces of Margie's apple pie on them. Everyone settled down. Les and Randy snuggled together in Les' big chair. Juan and Yancey sat next to each other on the couch, so close that with one move, Juan could be sitting on Yancey's lap.

"What's going on, Tony?" Les broke the uncomfortable silence.

"Angelina is divorcing Luis."

"It's about damn time," Juan shouted.

"Juan, watch your mouth." Brody admonished the younger man.

Tony stared at his nephew. "How long have you known about your uncle?"

"U-m-m..." Juan glanced at Yancey for help.

Yancey spoke up. "He didn't want to hurt his aunt's feelings."

Tony held up his hand, stopping any more words from spilling out of Yancey's mouth. "Let Juan do his own talking. We'll get to you soon enough."

Brody frowned, wondering what Tony knew. He settled back with his coffee mug, ready to watch the show.

"How long, Juan?" Tony asked again.

Juan stared down at the carpet. "Since before Thanksgiving."

"How did you find out?" Tony sat on the coffee table in front of the boys.

"It was the weekend of my birthday. My friends and I went to one of the clubs downtown. I saw Luis there. He was trying to pick a guy up..." Juan's voice tapered off.

"Did you know the guy?"

Brody had a feeling the guy was in the room with them.

"Luis was trying to pick me up." Yancey set his mug on the coffee table and glared at Tony. "I did stuff with him once, but that was before I knew he was Juan's uncle. The minute I found out, I refused to have anything else to do with the bastard."

Tony nodded. "I saw the look you exchanged when I told you Angelina was here to talk about Luis. He never forced you or hurt you in any way, did he, Yancey?"

Yancey shook his head. "No. He'd try to hassle me, but someone would come and rescue me." His blue eyes narrowed and he looked at Juan. "That wouldn't have been your doing, would it?"

Juan blushed. "Yeah, they were friends of mine. I'd asked them to keep an eye out and make sure *mi tío* didn't bother you."

Yancey sighed and took Juan's hand in his. "Thanks, but I could have dealt with it on my own."

"Your sister knows your brother-in-law cheats on her with men. She drove all the way up here from

Texas to ask you if you knew?" Randy looked surprised.

"Yes. It was the shock of seeing him with another guy. She confronted him and he said something about the fag spilling his guts. It's a toss-up which one of us he meant." Tony stood and moved behind Brody, rubbing his hand over Brody's shoulder.

"He never saw me at the clubs," Juan said. "I managed to stay out of his sight."

"So it was either Yancey or me." Tony tapped Brody's hand, bringing his attention to the dark haired man. "Remember the conversation we had a couple days ago about our first loves?"

Brody frowned and nodded. They had been talking about Yancey and Juan. "Yes."

"I told you my first love was the worst experience of my life and it scarred me." Tony reached over, grabbed the fork out of his hand and took a bite of his pie.

"Then you distracted me." Brody managed not to blush when he remembered how he'd been distracted.

"Luis was my first love."

"No shit?" Juan's jaw dropped open.

Brody carefully set his plate down and tugged his cowboy into his lap. He hugged Tony tight, whispering, "I thought he was an asshole before this. Now I know he is, along with being stupid. A smart man would've never let you go. Lucky for you, my momma always said I was the smartest son she had."

A shudder racked Tony's stocky body. Brody knew it'd been hard for him to tell them about Luis.

"It's in the past, love. You've got a new family here and we won't ever turn our backs on you." He kissed Tony hard and deep, claiming him. His cock hardened and began to ache. He wanted to do something to mark Tony as his.

"Does anyone else have any other earth-shattering secrets?" Les' amused voice broke through the fog of need threatening to overcome Brody's control.

Everyone shook their head.

"Then I suggest we go to bed. We can deal with everything in the morning."

Les stood before helping Randy to his feet, joining him. Both men smiled at Tony who stayed snuggled in Brody's arms.

"Brody's right, Tony. No matter what, you're a member of this family and nothing will ever change that. We've all known what it's like not to be wanted." Randy leaned over and brushed a kiss over Tony's cheek then gave Brody one as well.

Les nodded, squeezing their shoulders with a strong grip. Juan and Yancey said good night.

Brody stood, holding Tony in his arms, and for the first time, Tony didn't struggle to be set down. Revealing secrets had taken energy and Tony seemed to be willing to trust Brody to take care of him.

"Come on, love. Let's go to bed." He grinned at Tony. "I want to show you just how much you mean to me."

Chapter Seventeen

The next morning, Brody was sitting in the kitchen when Angelina came in.

"Coffee?"

He held up his mug and pointed to the pot resting on the counter near where he sat. She nodded, giving him a tentative smile. After reaching up, he grabbed another mug then filled it. He set it down on the table across from him.

"Have a seat. Would you like cream or sugar?" His words were stiff.

He was uncomfortable and unsure of how to act around Tony's sister. An image of Tony's family as monsters had been created in his mind, mostly from Tony's avoidance of discussing them.

"Black is fine. Have I missed breakfast?" She fidgeted with her mug.

"Of course not," Margie said, bustling in from the laundry room. "How about eggs and toast? Would you like some, Brody?"

"No, Margie. I'm fine."

"Please, I don't want to make more work for you," Angelina protested.

"It's no work at all, Ms Romanos. Those two youngsters will be coming back in, hungry again, so I can dish you out some of what I make them." Margie pulled out pots and skillets.

"Where's Tony?" Angelina asked Brody.

He looked up from the newspaper he'd been trying to read. "He was gone when I got up. I figured he was down at the bucking chutes working some of the rough stock Dusty and Burt are bringing along."

"Rough stock?"

Margie laughed. "It's like they're speaking a foreign language sometimes. It took me a long time to learn it, especially once Randy and Tony started living here. I was constantly asking them to interpret for me."

"Now she talks the lingo like the rest of us." Randy walked in with Juan and Yancey. "When she talks to one of the rodeo stock guys, they don't know she's one of those crazy East Coasters."

"Hush now, young man. If you don't want to wash my floors again, you'll take your boots off." Margie stood, glaring at them like a guard protecting her land.

"Sorry, Margie love." Randy gave her a kiss on his way to wash up in the sink. "We wouldn't want to ruin your hard work."

The younger men gave the elderly housekeeper hugs as they followed Randy's lead. Randy dried his hands before pouring some coffee then sitting down next to Brody.

"Tony said he'd be up in a few minutes. He had to finish talking with Dusty about one of the bulls." Randy's gaze skated over to Angelina.

Brody nodded. "I figured he wouldn't miss a chance at Margie's breakfast." He waved a hand towards Tony's sister. "Angelina Romanos, this is Randy Hersch. He and his partner, Les Hardin, are the owners of the ranch."

"Ma'am." Randy shook Angelina's hand.

"Nice to meet you." She looked at Juan. "No hug for your *Tía*?"

Juan studied her for a second then hugged her tight. "I'm sorry about *Tío* Luis, *Tía*."

"So am I, *mijo*, so am I." She gave Yancey a smile. "Who's your friend?"

"I'm Yancey MacCafferty, Ms Romanos. Brody's younger brother." Yancey nodded at her as he took his place at the table.

"Juan, why don't you help Margie put breakfast on the table," Brody suggested, figuring the teenager needed something to do. Turning to Randy, he asked, "Where's Les? I haven't seen him this morning."

"Had a bad night. I let him sleep in." Randy refilled everyone's mug. "There wasn't anything pressing for him to do."

"Good." Brody had come to worry about Les as much as everyone else did.

The door banged open and Tony strolled in. He lined his boots up with the others, but instead of washing up first, he walked over to Brody and kissed him.

"You were sleeping so soundly, I didn't want to wake you." Tony kissed him again.

"Thanks, baby." Brody stroked his cheek. "Go wash up so you can eat."

"Right." Tony whistled, heading to the sink. "How'd you sleep, Angelina?"

Brody shot a glance at Tony's sister. She had an uncomfortable look on her face, but at least it wasn't outright disgust. She'd better get used to guys kissing like that, he thought, because Les and Randy were worse than they were.

"Not bad. I talked to Mama and told her where I was. She didn't want to discuss my divorcing Luis. She seems to believe we can reconcile."

"*Abuela* really wants you to stay with *Tío* Luis, even though he's a cheater and gay?" Juan sounded puzzled.

"Mama's very traditional. When you marry someone, you marry them for life." Angelina sighed, a sad look on her face. "I guess I'm not willing to turn a blind eye."

Tony joined them and Juan served the food. Nothing was said for several minutes while everyone filled their stomachs. Brody sipped his coffee. This was one of his favourite times of the day. Everyone would gather around the table and make plans for the day.

"*Tía* Angelina," Juan said hesitantly. "How is my mom?"

"She's all right. Maria cries sometimes. I know she's hurt." Angelina gripped Juan's hand. "I want you to know that no matter how terrible I thought your being gay was, I never told her to disown you."

"You didn't?" Tony looked surprised. "I thought she talked to you and Luis."

"She did. Luis was the one who spoke of disowning Juan and throwing him out of the house. I was against it. No mother should ever turn their back on their child. Ever." The strength of her convictions rang in her voice.

"Yet you turned your back on Tony. Threw him away like a piece of garbage." Brody wasn't ready to forgive and forget.

Angelina had the decency to look embarrassed. She shifted in her seat, but Brody wasn't interested in giving her an out. No one else said anything.

"I know and I'm sorry for that. Things were different back then. I wouldn't have dreamed about going against Mama and Papa." Angelina looked up to see everyone staring at her. "I'm still not convinced it's something you can't help. I believe it's a choice."

"You believe the right girl could turn any of us straight?" Brody gestured to all the men at the table.

The stubborn tilt of Angelina's chin looked familiar.

"I have the right to my own beliefs."

"I thought you wanted to be a family again." Tony stared at her from where he sat next to Brody.

"I do. I believe it's a choice and not genetic, but that doesn't mean I'm going to try to change you." Angelina sighed. "I can learn to deal with who you love, Antonio. Man or woman. The only thing that matters is you love each other."

Brody nodded.

Tony's big sister smiled. "You don't need me to validate any of your feelings, Tony. Last night you told me you had a family here and I had to fit in with your family."

Tony leaned against Brody and he slid his arm around the man's waist, drawing him closer. Randy grinned and elbowed Yancey who took Juan's hand. It was obvious everyone in the room was there because they cared about each other.

"No matter what I think, I'm not going to call you names or act disgusted when you touch or kiss. I'll get used to all of it." She reached across the table to touch

Tony's hand. "Just give me a chance. I'm not too old to change."

"Mama and Papa?"

Brody's heart ached at the pain in Tony's voice. He pulled his cowboy closer to him.

Angelina shook her head. "I wouldn't bet on them opening up to you again, *mi hermano*. They haven't spoken of you in years. I'll do what I can to bend them. You know what they're like."

"Rigid," Juan murmured.

"Traditional," Tony said at the same time.

"Neither of those means they won't change their minds," Brody pointed out. "Just that it'll be harder for them to move beyond the boundaries they set for themselves."

Jackson walked in as silence fell over them. He glanced around at all the serious faces. "Did someone die?"

"No. We're talking about families." Yancey poured some juice into Juan's glass.

"Really? Mine doesn't usually tend to make me sad," Jackson joked as he filled his plate.

"Your family isn't like ours." Tony shifted.

"That's true. They're straight." Jackson ducked a piece of toast Randy threw at him. "I caught the weather report a few minutes ago. There's a storm rolling in. It should hit later this afternoon. If you're going to fly out tonight, Brody, you'll want to head down to Cheyenne now."

"Fuck." Brody didn't want to think about flying back to L.A., but he needed to get home.

"I'll drive you down there," Randy offered.

"No." Tony shook his head. "Angelina needs to get home. I'll ride back with her. We can drop Brody off in Cheyenne on the way to Texas."

"Should I come with you, *Tío*?" Juan looked like he was hoping Tony would say no.

"No point to it—and you have school." Tony pulled away from Brody and stood. "Clean up the kitchen while we pack."

Breakfast was over. Jackson caught Randy and they left, talking about the horses. Juan and Yancey started cleaning off the table, and Angelina helped them. Brody and Tony headed to their room.

As soon as the door had shut them in the room, Brody encircled Tony's waist with his arm and jerked the man tight to him. Their mouths met in a rough kiss. He bit Tony's bottom lip then soothed the sting with his tongue. Tony grabbed Brody's ass and squeezed.

They broke off the kiss when his lungs burned for air. Brody grinned at Tony and started unbuttoning the man's shirt.

"What are you doing?" Tony didn't seem to care if Brody answered or not. His fingers were undoing Brody's buckle.

"You weren't around when I woke up this morning. Didn't get to give you my usual morning hello."

He pushed Tony's shirt down from his broad shoulders and tugged Tony's white T-shirt off. Leaning down, he licked the dusky brown nipple in front of him. Tony groaned, his hands faltering on Brody's zipper.

"I'm not sure we have time."

Brody pulled back enough to blow a puff of air over Tony's wet flesh. "Baby, we always have time for this."

"Ah."

He liked Tony this way, caught up in the moment and his mind not working. Kneeling, he stripped

Tony's jeans down. Tony put his hands on Brody's shoulders, bracing while Brody pulled the fabric over his feet. He flung the pants to the side and focused on the hard cock standing proud in front of him.

The tip of the shaft was red and glistened with pre-cum. Tony rocked forward, brushed Brody's lips and seemed to beg for attention. Brody licked his lips and grinned as he barely touched his tongue to Tony's head.

"Brody. Please."

He ran his hands up Tony's lightly furred calves and thighs, teasing the crease where Tony's hips and legs met. Gripping Tony's hips, he leant forward and wrapped his mouth around the crown of Tony's dick. Slowly as possible, he sucked Tony's shaft in until his nose burrowed into the dark curls at the base of Tony's cock. Brody hummed as it hit the back of his throat.

"Fuck," Tony groaned, trying to move while Brody kept him still.

He pressed Tony's hips back against the door and shook his head. Working his mouth up and down Tony's dick, he kept the suction steady and hard. Brody wrapped one of his hands around the bottom section of the shaft and pumped. He slid his other hand down between Tony's legs, caressing the soft skin behind Tony's balls.

Tony shivered, his entire body shaking. Brody pulled off until just the head was in his mouth. He laved it with his tongue, flicking the spongy flesh and slipping the tip of his tongue into the slit. Tony's head hit the door with a thud.

Brody fumbled with the zipper of his own jeans. He wanted to get them open before he came. He fisted his own cock and started stroking, moaning around

Tony's shaft. He moved his other hand off Tony's dick to tease his lover's puckered hole.

"Brody."

His name was strangled in Tony's throat. He took Tony in again, deep-throating him and swallowing around his length. Tony jerked and swore. Brody thrust his finger into Tony's passage and nailed his gland with his knuckle.

He couldn't understand what Tony shouted as the cowboy came, flooding his mouth with salty bitter cum. He drank it down and he came, his own spunk coating his hand. Brody took everything Tony gave him, pulling away only when Tony stopped moving. He nuzzled the softening dick and cleaned it with his tongue.

Brody climbed to his feet, leaning in to kiss Tony. His cowboy lifted his covered hand and licked the cum off. After his hand was back to pre-sex cleanliness, he kissed Tony again, tasting his own essence in the man's mouth.

"We should straighten up and head out."

He nodded. Brody had hoped to have more time with Tony, but there was no way of knowing how bad the storm would get. He couldn't stay any longer. His partners had set up several important meetings for later in the week.

"You're right. Let's go."

* * * *

Later that night, Tony flung himself onto the hotel bed and groaned. He hated driving, especially through a storm that seemed to be following him. He tossed his hat on the desk, adhering to the old tradition of no hats on the bed. He didn't want bad luck. He tugged his phone out of his jacket pocket, then checked his voicemails. The first one was Randy making sure they were okay and asking him to call. The storm had been worse back at the ranch.

Brody had left him a message, letting him know he'd landed safely. He smiled and hit speed dial.

"Hey there, sweet cheeks."

Brody's voice danced over Tony's skin, making goose bumps rise.

"Blondie, how's it going?" he teased.

"Good. Came into the office for a while. Straightening things up. Waiting for my partners to get here."

Tony caught a hint of tension in Brody's tone.

"Trouble in paradise?" He grabbed a pillow and stuffed it behind his head.

"There might be when I tell them I'm moving."

This time excitement mixed with the tension.

"Moving? You found a place?"

"Not sure. I called the agent as soon as I landed. She's found a place a couple of miles down the road from Les'." Brody laughed. "I told Yancey to take the guys with him to check it out since you weren't around."

"When are they going?" He fought his own excitement.

They'd looked at several ranches. There had been something wrong with each of them, besides not being as close as they wanted to their friends.

"The storm's over up there, but they won't be able to drive until tomorrow."

Tony could hear the creak of the chair when Brody shifted.

"Even if this ends up being another dead end, Morgan and Vance should know I'm planning on leaving the state."

"Good idea, babe."

A knock sounded on his hotel door.

"Angelina's ready to head out for dinner. Lucky for us, there's a diner attached to this place."

He levered his aching body off the bed, put his hat on and opened the door.

"Good. Morgan just arrived. I'll talk to you tomorrow. Sweet dreams, love."

Brody hung up before Tony could process what the man had said. When it did, he stared at the phone in surprise.

They'd never used that word to each other or to describe how they felt. It had been implied for a month or two, but he hadn't felt the need to say it. Now Brody had broken their unspoken agreement by uttering that four-letter word.

Tony wanted to call Brody back and yet he didn't. Stupid really. Saying the word wouldn't ruin what they had. Maybe it would make it a little more real.

"Anything wrong?" Angelina studied him as he gathered his room key and followed her out into the hall.

"No."

It was unexpected, but everything was okay.

* * * *

Los Angeles

"You're fucking kidding," Morgan shouted.

Brody watched his business partner and friend pace their office. "No, I'm not. I want to move."

Morgan shot him a shocked glance. "Why?"

"I'm tired of this city. I'm tired of the attitudes." He spun his chair around and stared out of the window at the Hollywood sign.

"It's that cowboy. What's his name?" Morgan frowned and snapped his fingers. "Tony. You're moving to a ranch because of that bull rider."

"Yes and no. I love Tony. We've spent as much time as we can together. We talk every day." He held up his hand to stop Morgan's next words. "It's also because of Yancey. He likes it out in Wyoming. He's got a good steady life out there and I want to be a part of it."

"You can be a part of it without moving there. Why Wyoming, Mac?" Morgan gestured wildly. "You can pick any state. Why there?"

"It's where they want to be."

His decision was as simple as that. Tony and Yancey both loved Wyoming. He loved them. His life was ready for a change.

"You and Vance can run the bodyguard part of the company from here. I'll handle the security systems from Wyoming. We'll meet when we need to."

"Your mind's made up." Morgan sighed.

"Yes. I wanted to tell you before I found a place, but I am moving. This isn't home for me anymore."

"And Tony is?" Morgan perched on the edge of Brody's desk.

Brody was quiet for a minute. "Yes, he is. I wasn't looking for someone. Figured it would happen in its own good time. Now that it has, I'm ready for something new. Somewhere different."

Morgan's intense grey eyes focused on him and Brody didn't fidget or look away. Finally, his friend grinned.

"We'll have papers drawn up for a branch office in Wyoming. Maybe we could set up a training facility out there as well for our guards. We'll have to hash out a schedule and division of power that works for all of us." Morgan came around the desk to slap Brody on the shoulder. "I knew it would happen."

Brody frowned. "What would happen?"

"You'd fall for someone, but I always thought it'd be some twink or wannabe actor. I didn't know you went for rugged cowboy types."

He shot to his feet and gave Morgan a hug. "I didn't think they were my type either, but you've met him, Morgan. Maybe it's that little hint of vulnerability he covers with all that fierce confidence."

"I know what you mean. Come on. Let's grab Vance and head to dinner. We need to tell him about our decisions. Afterwards, we can head to the club. Celebrate the end of your swinging single days and the start of a new step forward for the company."

After grabbing his coat, Brody walked out of the office. His revelation had gone well. He could only hope Tony's meeting with his parents went as smoothly.

Chapter Eighteen

Texas
Thursday

Tony pulled into his parents' driveway. They still lived in the same house Tony had grown up in. Nothing had changed. Same colour of paint. Same flowers. Even the same car, just a newer model.

He shook his head. His parents were stuck in their happy narrow world. He wasn't sure he wanted to challenge it.

His mother stood on the front steps, frowning at them as they walked towards her.

"*Mija*, you shouldn't have run away. You must talk to *tu marido*. Luis is *muy afligido* for what he did."

"Saying he's sorry doesn't make everything okay, Mama." Angelina shook her head. "He cheated on me, more than once."

"If you would be a better wife, he wouldn't feel the need to find comfort elsewhere."

Mama continued to ignore Tony, which didn't bother him as much as he'd thought it would.

"No, Mama. This isn't my fault. I loved Luis. I did everything he wanted. He's been cheating since we married." Angelina gestured to Tony. "He admitted it to Antonio. Luis doesn't consider it cheating because it's men he sleeps with."

Tony felt his mother's disgust and anger hit him like physical blows when she turned her dark gaze on him.

"He isn't welcome, Angelina. How dare you go against our wishes and bring him here."

He set his chin. No way was he going to react to his mother's cruel words.

"Antonio's not here for you, Mama. He's here because he wanted to make sure I got home all right." Angelina placed her hand on Tony's arm.

Mama crossed her arms and glared at them. "He's not a part of this family anymore. He turned his back on us when he chose that vile lifestyle and to live in sin. Now he's corrupted Juan."

A harsh laugh burst from him. "How could I have corrupted Juan when the first time I talked to him was last November?"

Angelina shook her head, but he was tired of being silent. Why should he be worried about upsetting his mother when she didn't give a damn how much her words hurt him?

Mama narrowed her eyes. "Don't talk to me like that. I'm your mother. You show me some respect."

"I'll show you respect when you respect me. You're not my mother. You've been very clear on that point." Tony studied her and every moment of guilt and shame he'd felt disappeared.

He handed the keys to his sister and hugged her. "You know where to find me if you need to talk."

"Let me drive you to the airport." She grabbed at him.

He stepped away. "You need to talk to Mama." He smiled. "I need to leave. This isn't home for me, *mi hermana,* and I'm not going to beg them to make me a part of the family again."

She shot a look over her shoulder at their mother, who was trying to act like she wasn't listening, and grimaced. "I don't blame you. You don't belong here. Wyoming's the perfect place for you and Juan, with people who love you." She hugged him.

"Thanks. Take care, Angelina." He nodded, picked up his bags and headed down the driveway.

He'd call a cab when he got farther from the house. He'd walked away before, but this time he wasn't running from something. There was a whole group of people waiting for him.

After reaching the corner, he called the cab then dialled Brody's number.

"Tony. Everything okay?"

A warm feeling raced through him. It was nice to know Brody was concerned for him.

"Yeah, everything's better than okay."

He looked back at his parents' house. Angelina and his mother were still out front yelling at each other.

"Have you heard from Yancey yet about the ranch?"

"Not yet, but they should be looking at it right now."

Tony knew Brody was curious about what had happened when Tony saw his mother, but his lover wasn't going to ask him.

"Great. You better make sure there's room enough for at least one other person." He held his breath.

"You'll move in with me when I get a place?"

"I will. Not sure what was stopping me from agreeing to it in the first place. I mean, I love you, Brody. Makes sense for us to live together." He bit his bottom lip. Strange how nervous he could get just by saying that word.

Brody laughed. "I love you, too. Not exactly how I planned on telling you, though."

"Yeah. Me standing on a street corner waiting for a cab and you halfway across the country."

The cab pulled up in front of him.

"Hey, my ride's here. I'll call you tonight and we'll talk about that place." He handed his bags to the driver.

"Sure. Take care and have a safe flight, love."

"Bye, baby."

After hanging up, he tucked his phone in his pocket. Happiness was a feeling he liked. He was on his way to ride bulls and he had a man who loved him. What more could he ask for?

* * * *

Wyoming
Monday

Tony climbed out of the truck, taking his time. God, his body ached. The first event back after an injury was always the roughest. He grinned at Jackson, who had picked him up from the airport.

Juan dashed out of the main house. "*Tío* Tony, are you okay?"

"Aside from being sore and stiff, I'm fine." Tony threw an arm around Juan and hugged him.

Juan smiled and hugged him back. "Glad to hear that. I didn't like getting the call from Brody last time you rode."

"Understandable. Help me out, kid and grab my bags for me." He gestured to the back seat of the truck's cab.

Juan pulled the bags out while Jackson unloaded some feed bags.

"Thanks for picking me up," Tony said to the foreman.

"No problem." Jackson lifted two bags on his shoulder and headed towards the training barn.

Tony followed his nephew into the house. He settled in a recliner in the living room, staring at the fire that was burning cheerfully. March was still chilly enough to justify a fire. Juan joined him after he'd dropped Tony's bags in his room.

"Where's Yancey?" He noticed Brody's younger brother didn't seem to be around.

"He went to the horse show with Les and Randy." Juan pouted. "I had to go to school."

"It sucks, doesn't it?" He smiled at Juan.

"What does?" Juan's blush told Tony the kid knew what he was getting at.

"Not having him around."

"Yeah, but it has to be worse for you. I mean Brody's in California. It's not like he lives close by. At least I know Yancey'll be back in a few days." Juan lay on the couch, eyes closed and hands behind his head.

"True." Tony fidgeted with his shirt sleeve for a second. "What if I told you Brody's looking for a ranch around here?"

"Really? That would be awesome. We could see them whenever we wanted." Juan's face lit up with joy.

"What would you say if I told you Brody wants us to move in with him and Yancey when they find a place?" He shrugged. "I already told him I would."

Juan sat up, a look of surprise on his face. "No shit?"

"No shit." Tony leaned his head back on the chair and closed his eyes. He entwined his fingers together. "It's weird thinking I might end up with a home. It was the one thing I thought I gave up when I ran away all those years ago."

He felt Juan's hand on his good shoulder.

"You always have a place here. You know Les and Randy would never throw you out."

He pushed to his feet and sighed. "I know, but I want a place that's mine. Where I'm not a third wheel. No matter how open they are, Randy and Les only need each other for true happiness." Tony scrubbed his face with his hand. "I'm tired. I'm going to bed. Don't stay up too late."

Juan rolled his eyes at him and Tony chuckled.

It was good to be back, even though he missed Brody. He had a feeling it wouldn't be long before they found a home of their own.

Chapter Nineteen

Las Vegas, Nevada, PBR Finals
Eight months later

"God, harder."

Brody hooked his ankles together around Tony's waist, his heels digging into Tony's ass. He rocked his hips and pushed down into each of Tony's thrusts.

Tony's thick shaft stroked in and out, the spongy head pegging Brody's gland each time. Brody's hands were pressed against the wall above the bed, keeping him from hitting his head as Tony fucked him hard and fast.

He clenched his inner passage, massaging Tony's cock and encouraging his lover to come. Brody's eyes rolled when Tony gripped his aching dick and pumped.

"Shit," Tony moaned as Brody bucked underneath him.

Brody couldn't say anything. He'd lost all ability to speak or think the moment rough skin had enveloped his dick.

Overwhelmed by the sensations of his climax building, he might have whimpered. Lightning danced along his spine and struck, tingling and hot in his balls.

Brody exploded, painting their stomachs, chests and Tony's hand with thick white strings of cum. Drifting on the pleasure of his own release, he barely registered Tony's at first.

Tony jerked and froze. He remained buried in Brody's ass while he emptied a flood of hot cum into Brody. Brody undulated, milking every last drop from Tony's cock.

He grunted as Tony's solid weight landed on his chest. He let his legs drop to either side of Tony's hips. Running his fingers down Tony's sweat-covered spine, he kissed Tony's forehead.

"Relaxed now?"

Tony mumbled something.

Brody nudged him. "Can't understand you, babe."

"I'm so relaxed, I think I'll take a nap."

He chuckled. "Sorry, love. We're meeting everyone in thirty minutes for lunch before you head over to the Thomas and Mack to get ready."

"Damn," Tony grumbled, rolling over onto his back. "Do we at least have time for a shower?"

"If we're quick." Brody hesitated before saying, "Angelina called last night. She's planning on watching today. Said to wish you good luck."

"I appreciate the call."

He caught a hint of sarcasm in Tony's voice.

"She's trying. Between your parents and that bastard husband of hers, she's going crazy. Maybe she'll be able to come next year."

Tony sighed. "You're right. I'll call her tonight after I win."

"No lack of confidence here, I see." He slapped Tony on the hip and climbed out of bed. "Let's go before they come looking for us."

"Don't you think I'll ride my last two bulls and win?"

"Of course I do, sweetheart." He winked at Tony. "I have the utmost confidence in your ability."

* * * *

Four hours later, Brody's confidence was severely shaken when he found out what bull Tony was to ride in the Championship round.

"You're not riding that bull." Brody stalked up to Tony.

Tony turned and glared at him. Brody realised he'd challenged his lover in front of Tony's fellow riders. He gritted his teeth.

"Can I talk to you somewhere else?"

Tony nodded, said something to the others and led the way to a small, deserted hallway. Brody followed, not caring if Les and Randy were keeping up or not.

As soon as they were alone, Brody grabbed Tony's arm and pulled him around. "You're not riding that bull, Tony," he commanded.

"I have to ride." Tony didn't jerk away, but took Brody's hand in a tight grip.

"You're hurt and that bastard is the most dangerous bull on tour. If healthy cowboys can't stay on him, what makes you think you can?" Brody wasn't questioning Tony's riding ability. He was worried about the condition of Tony's shoulder. Tony had injured his right shoulder in the last round. It was the arm he held onto the bull rope with.

"I have to ride him, love." Tony kept his voice low. "If I make eight on him, I'll win the Finals and the championship. I've been working for this all my life, Brody. I can't walk away from this."

"But he's psychotic. He can do serious damage." Brody touched Tony's cheek, fighting the need to take the cowboy in his arms.

"I know that. I helped carry Cody out of the arena when that asshole slab of meat stomped him into the dirt. That bull should be put down, but I can't worry about that. I have to ride. Don't you understand?" Tony pleaded.

Brody shook his head, turning away. He saw Les and Randy standing a little way down the hall. He pointed at Randy.

"Explain to him why he shouldn't do this."

Les shrugged and Randy shook his head. The younger man stepped forward.

"I was never a rodeo junkie. It was a way for me to make money, but I'm not going to try and convince Tony to withdraw. One ride and he wins." Randy grinned at Tony. "Go for it."

Randy hugged Tony and gave Brody an apologetic smile. He appealed to Les, who touched his shoulder.

"Sometimes you have to let them go after something they want. No matter how scared you are." Les pulled Randy farther down the hall. "Give Tony a hug and a kiss. Wish him good luck. He needs to get back out there and we need to go to our seats."

Brody stared down at his feet. Fear and panic swamped him. He wanted to fall to his knees and beg Tony not to make that ride. The night Cody had ended up in intensive care because of that bull, Brody had gone back to the hotel room and had thrown up. He'd never been so scared of what Tony did for a living.

Tony touched his hand and lifted his chin so they could look at each other.

"I have to do this, love."

Brody wrapped his arms around Tony's waist, burying his face against the bull rider's neck. "I know. I'm sorry. Your job worries me, but I can usually deal with it. That bull fucking scares me to death, baby."

Tony embraced him and held him tight. Those scarred, callused hands Brody loved so much smoothed up and down his back.

"I know you're afraid and any person in their right mind would be of that bull. But I'm not."

Brody jerked away, staring at him as if he'd just announced he was pregnant.

"You're kidding, right?"

Tony grasped Brody's shoulders. "No, I'm not kidding. Oh, I'm afraid. It's the same fear I feel every time I get on a bull, but I can ride him. I've studied every tape I could find on him. I've talked to every cowboy who has ever been on his back. I knew it was only a matter of time before I drew him at an event." Tony grinned. "I figured I would get him here for sure. He's a championship-round bull and I'm the leader going into the short go. Trust me. I can do it." He brushed a soft kiss over Brody's mouth. "Believe me. I need to know you're behind me."

Brody kissed him back. "If you say you can do it, I trust you can."

"Thank you." He hugged his partner tight.

"Tony, they're starting. We need to get back to our seats before Juan and Yancey come looking for us." Les stuck his head around the corner.

"We're coming."

Thirty minutes later, Tony watched them run Tank's Reward into the chute. The bull was big—one of the biggest on the tour. Pure black with horns two feet wide on each side of his head. Tony had watched all the tapes he could find on Tank and he knew how the bull used those horns as weapons.

A rope was threaded through the top rails. Tank had a tendency to rear in the chute, slamming riders into the metals gates around them. Tony dropped his rope on the right side of the bull. He saw that black hide twitch. The gate man hooked the end and pulled it under Tank's stomach.

Tank tossed his head, almost catching one cowboy with a horn. Tony eased down on the bull's back and gestured for one of the riders to start pulling his rope tight. Tank snorted as the bull felt the first pinch of the rigging around his stomach. Tony trusted the other men around the chute to save him if Tank decided to rear.

He wrapped the tail of his rope tight around his gloved hand. Folding his fingers over it, he tested his grip. It was as solid as he could get. He pushed his hat on, shooting a glance up into the seats where he knew his family sat. Brody was standing, his fists clenched and his face pale. Tony gave Brody a wink, and Brody nodded back.

Tony looked back down and noticed Tank's Reward had tilted his head in such a way, Tony could tell the bull was studying him. That black eye rimmed with white rolled. Rage burned in that gaze. A demon lived inside the bull and all Tank wanted was to destroy the creature trying to control him.

Tony understood fury because he'd lived with it for a long time. The same fury that made Tony the best bull rider in the world made Tank's Reward the best bull in the world.

"Ladies and gentlemen, this is the ride we've been waiting for. Tony Romanos, first in the Finals standings and first in overall points, is matched against Tank's Reward. Tank has been out forty-three times and never been ridden. If you looked up the meaning of the word 'rank', you'd see a picture of this bull," the announcer said. "All Romanos has to do is stay on for eight seconds, but that, folks, is easier said than done."

Tony said a silent prayer and nodded. Tank's Reward exploded from the chute. Something tore in Tony's shoulder. The pain was so overwhelming, he almost passed out. He bit his lip and held on, even though he could feel his grip getting weaker. The bull bucked, trying to bring Tony down over his head. When that didn't work, the beast reversed and started spinning, using the speed of the circles to drop Tony into the well where Tank could hook a horn into him.

Chaz, one of the bullfighters, darted by, catching Tony's eye. Tony heard the buzzer, signalling the end of the ride and reached for the tail of his rope. The one thing he didn't want to do was hang up. That would cause more damage to his shoulder and he risked getting stomped by Tank's Reward.

His hand came free and he started looking for a place to get off. Tony couldn't feel his shoulder anymore. Fred raced past, getting the bull to flatten out and stop spinning long enough for Tony to bail.

His feet hit the dirt and Tony raced to the fence. He didn't know where Tank's Reward was, but he wasn't going to look around. Scrambling up the metal railing one-armed, he felt a hot breeze brush past his legs.

Glancing down, he saw the hindquarters of that black bull go by.

Tony searched the stands. Yancey and Juan were jumping and yelling. Les and Randy both grinned at him. He met Brody's gaze. His lover's face held worry, but pride and love shone in his eyes. A simple tip of the hat to Brody and he climbed down to the arena floor. The bullfighters came running up to him. One of them carried his rope. He reached out and fell to his knees.

Pain shot through his body. He held his arm with his good hand and groaned. Blackness filled his vision.

Epilogue

Wyoming
One week later

Brody walked to meet Tony in front of his truck. He slid an arm around the stocky bull rider's waist, making sure he didn't jostle Tony's arm. Brody stroked his fingers over the championship buckle Tony wore.

Tony leaned into him, his right arm supported in a sling. They looked at the white ranch house. Brody heard the boys climbing out of the truck. Yancey and Juan came to join them.

"This is it?" Tony smiled.

"Yep. Les and I checked it out while you were in the hospital and then he took care of all the papers for us. It's ours."

Les and Randy stepped out onto the large stone porch. Randy smiled at them. "Are you coming? There's a whole bunch of people here to throw you a house-warming party."

Yancey and Juan raced up the steps and into the house. Tony saw how Yancey kept an eye on Juan to make sure the younger man was careful.

"I don't think it's puppy love." Tony shook his head. "I don't want them settling down with each other just yet. They both need to see the world and live life before they commit to each other."

"How are you going to keep them apart if we're all living in the same house?" Brody frowned.

Tony could tell Brody didn't like the idea of separating the boys. "I'm not going to keep them apart. I think their own interests will do that for a while. Yancey's heading back to college and Juan has to finish up high school yet. That'll keep them busy for a time while they grow up."

Brody turned, pulling Tony close to him, and bent to kiss him.

Tony savoured the smoky taste of the whisky Brody'd had on the aeroplane. He swept his tongue over the sensitive spot behind Brody's front teeth. His lover shivered.

"Hey, you two, quit that. You've got impressionable kids here," Les called from the porch.

They broke apart, chuckling. Tony shot Les the bird.

"We weren't doing anything either of them haven't seen before."

"Let's go. We'll pick up where we left off later." Brody headed in.

He followed, then stopped on the porch to look out over the land he co-owned with Brody. The green grass was spread out before him with the Rocky Mountains acting as a majestic backdrop.

Tony stood there, remembering all the homes he'd passed through during his life. Some had been harder to leave than others, but he always had, searching for something else.

Laughter drew him into the house. He stepped into the living room and saw his friends standing there. Brody blew him a kiss and Tony knew he'd finally found someone to love and a home to call his own.

About the Author

There is beauty in every kind of love, so why not live a life without boundaries? Experiencing everything the world offers fascinates TA and writing about the things that make each of us unique is how she shares those insights. When not writing, TA's watching movies, reading and living life to the fullest.

T.A. Chase loves to hear from readers. You can find her contact information, website details and author profile page at http://www.total-e-bound.com.

Total-E-Bound Publishing

www.total-e-bound.com

Take a look at our exciting range of literagasmic™
erotic romance titles and discover pure quality
at Total-E-Bound.